REPAIRMAN'S BLUES

GOOD SAMARITAN MYSTERY # 4

By

JAMES M. COURNEYA

THANKS

This book is for my family.
Barbara, Matt, Anna, and James

TABLE OF CONTENTS

THE CRAP HITS THE FAN

PICKING UP THE PIECES

REPAIRING THE MESS

HELPING THE NEEDY

THE NEW GUY

Sam, I mean me, felt great. The morning was bright and cheery. Nothing out of the ordinary had happened for almost a year. Joey was a few months from graduating. Marie had led the high school team to state in the fall. David was just finishing pre-school. Some days it felt like Jude and I were still in the honeymoon phase. Sure, a lot of this had to do with the streak of bad things ending, so I felt great.

Walking through the doors at Good Sam's on a sunny day made me feel great to be alive. The crew was busy prepping the store for the morning's opening. Linda spotted me as soon as I walked in. She made a bee-line towards me.

"Just the man that I wanted to see."

"That sounds ominous. What do you need on this fine day?"

"Nothing too ominous, but I would like you to talk with Doug about the mess that he leaves in the store when he brings appliances into the store after hours. We have to clean up messes at least a couple times a week."

"Why aren't you speaking to him about the problem?" Linda stared at me with laser beam eyes. Oops, I must have hit a sore spot.

"Really, I have spoken to him more times than I can recall. You fix it or you might have a very unhappy store manager on your hands." I've stepped in it now.

"I will take care of it today. I'm sorry, I didn't mean to imply that you hadn't handled it."

"Take care of it. I'll think about whether I'll accept your apology." With that she turned and walked away.

Doug Toms was our new appliance repairman and trainer. Something was a touch off about his personality. I didn't have any problem with him, but the rest of the crew complained about his attitude. He was a good appliance guy, but he acted like picking up his messes was beneath him. This morning, I would speak to him when he showed up. I headed to my office to start my day and lick my wounds.

At around ten, I had a knock on my door. To my surprise, it was my son Joey.

"Joey, what brings you by this morning?"

"Dad, do you have a few minutes to talk?"

"Sure, have a seat." Joey came in and sat by my desk. I was very curious to find out what he needed.

"At school this morning, the seniors were meeting with the counselors about our post high school plans. I sent an application to the community college, but I thought that I needed to talk to you about all of my plans. I want to start at the community college and transfer to a four-year school to finish. I don't want to put too much of a burden on you and mom, so I figured that I need some type of work ability that I can use anywhere. I would like to apply for the appliance repair apprenticeship here. I can do the work and still go to classes. I hope that the spot isn't filled yet?"

"Well, to start with, it seems that you've put a lot of thought into your future. The spot is not filled, so I'll get the paperwork for you. You can fill them out now or at home. If you have time, I'll take you back to meet Doug our trainer."

"That would be great, dad. I don't have to be back before noon."

We took a leisurely walk back to the appliance repair shop. Doug looked like he was hard at work. I know that I promised Linda to speak to Doug, but it would have to wait until I was done with Joey.

"Do you have a minute?" Doug turned to me and smiled.

"Sure, I always have time for the boss."

"Great, I'd like to introduce you to my son, Joey." Joey was kind of hanging back as Doug gave him his hand.

"Nice to meet you, Joey." The two shook hands.

"I would like to talk to you about the apprentice program."

"Oh, I thought you were going to tell me about Linda's complaint. I'll try to do better. I don't notice that I've made a mess. Tell her that I'm sorry." Doug had an odd grin while he talked.

"I'll let her know. Back to the program, my son would like to apply so that he can afford college. If you could give him an overview of what to expect, I would appreciate it."

Joey and Doug began looking through the materials that they would cover in the program. Joey had to take a few classes at the college to complete the course. If he finished the course, he would be able to work as a certified repairman. As he took the course he would work part-time for Good Sam's. This would give him a job and pocket money as he completed his degree. I think that is a winner all around. I wandered around the shop. It had been a while since I've checked the room out. Doug started working for Good Sam's about a year ago. Ross our long-time appliance guy had retired due to health issues. It took a while to find a replacement with the required credentials.

"Joey, it has been a pleasure meeting you. I hope you decide to sign up for the apprentice position. I'm never out of work for long. I've met some great people over dead appliances."

"Thanks for taking time to talk to me, Mr. Toms."

"Call me Doug." We headed back to my office.

"That answered most of my questions, thanks, Dad. I have to get back to school." My oldest vanished out the door.

"Joey is looking so grown up. I can't believe that he's ready for college." Linda was smiling so; I must have been forgiven.

"You can't believe it, join the club. By the way, Doug brought up the subject, he told me to apologize to you for his messes. He claims that he doesn't notice them."

"Just so he stops leaving them, thank you Bossman." Hopefully, crisis averted.

The rest of the day traveled along a normal pattern. Customers and phone calls. Around four, a woman came in looking for the appliance guy. She couldn't remember his name, but had come in to look at washers and dryers. I paged Doug. He didn't respond. I showed her the available sets in the store. She liked some of the sets, yet she was hesitant to commit to buying until she talked to Doug.

"Can you give me your name and number? I'll pass them to Doug when he comes in tomorrow."

"Yeah, that will be okay, but I really wanted to take care of it today." She was acting very nervous as she we exchanged the information. When she finished, she handed me the paper and huffed out the door.

"Did you lose your touch? She looked a little bit peeved as she left."

"I don't know what that was about. After Doug didn't respond, she seemed agitated. Would you ask Bob if he can see if Doug is gone?"

"I'll check on it myself." Linda headed to the warehouse to check on Doug. She came back a few minutes later.

"Was he there?"

"No, the crew said that he left not too long after you and Joey went to talk to him. That's not very unusual for him. He kind of comes and goes."

"I'll catch him in the morning."

As I walked in the door, David ran to greet me. "Daddio, we're having company for dinner. Mom says to get washed up and help her in the kitchen." I'm sure the people living two blocks over heard his announcement.

"Tell Mom, that I'll be right in." David ran off to make his next announcement. It didn't take me long to wash up and join Jude in the kitchen.

"Can you give me a hand? Ginger is coming for dinner. Please, vacuum the front room."

"Sure, what do you need after that?"

"I'll think of something when you're done." I got the vacuum out of the hall closet and went to work. Just as I was finishing, Joey, Marie, and Ginger walked in.

"Grab your camera, Dad's doing housework."

"Funny, Marie, very funny." Marie and I headed to the kitchen, Joey and Ginger went into the family room.

"Marie, you're home, good. Can you help me, while your Dad sets the table?" I must be out of the loop. Ginger comes to dinner a couple nights a week; I wonder what all the fuss is today? I'm always the last to know.

Dinner was soon ready. Everyone gathered around the formal dining room table. Jude had produced a splendid looking feast. It reminded me that it had been a long time since lunch. The conversation was light as we ate. I looked around the room, realizing that my family was growing up. The feast was soon consumed. The table cleared, but everyone remained seated. Joey, finally looked up to start the conversation.

"Dad, I'd like to expand on our conversation this morning. Ginger and I have been doing a lot of thinking and talking about our futures. We think that it is important to share our plans with our families."

"I think that's a good idea. I take it there is more to your plans than what we discussed at work."

"Yes, a lot more. We want all of you to know what and why we're doing this."

Ginger spoke up. "We have both applied to White River College. We believe that it will help us be able to afford to finish school. After we get our Associates Degrees, we plan on transferring to best university that we can afford."

"So far, this sounds great. We'll help as much as we can." Jude and I had already talked about what we could contribute to each kids schooling.

"We have made up our minds to get married after we get our two-year degrees. That is why I came to talk to you today. I want to use the appliance repair certificate, so that I can pay most of our expenses. Even when we go to the university, I can still make money on the side."

"Most of what you've said is pretty clear, but are you two going to live together while going to White River?"

"No. we had hoped to stay at home, but paying rent for those years."

"Joey, Ginger, I think that is very doable on our part. What do your parents say about these plans?"

"They seem to be onboard, mostly because we aren't planning on living together before we get married. They're excited about me going to college with an idea about what I want out of it. Neither of them finished school. They said it was a lack of a plan and getting married before they were done."

"Joey, what are you planning to major in?"

"Dad, either teaching or business. I want to take classes in both to see what I like. I've watched you all these years and it intrigues me, but teaching and coaching, you know working with kids would be fulfilling, too!"

"Jeeze, Joey, I'm proud of you. A man with a plan. Ginger, you must be doing something right." Marie was looking at her brother and future sister-in-law with admiration.

"Jude, what do you think?" Jude waited a few seconds before answering.

"I think that it is very mature of both of you. As a mom, I think the plans have a chance of working. Waiting to get married is a good idea, not because I disapprove, but because it will let you finish school and land on your feet."

"Let us know when you get back information from the school. We're not so ancient that we can't help you through the process. Things like financial aid are sometimes tricky to navigate. I give it my blessing. We'll work on the other details as we stumble over them."

There was a look of relief on both their faces. I felt some relief, too, Joey and Ginger had stepped up to the plate and got a hit planning for their futures. Joey and Ginger said their goodbyes, before Joey drove her home.

"I didn't have time to tell you that Joey came by the store this morning. He talked to me about part of his plans. I introduced him to Doug. They went over what the appliance program would include. He seemed pretty sure of what he wanted. I hope that they follow through on their plans."

"He seemed so grown-up as they went through the plans. I was impressed."

"Me too, me too." I sat quietly taking in all of the day's announcements. My biggest wish for my children is that they do something that makes them happy. Ginger certainly makes Joey happy. I hope his career choices will bring that type of happiness. I know that a lot can change in two years. I never had all of my first choices come out like I envisioned them. Joey is smart. I believe he'll do okay.

IS HE REAL OR NOT?

I stepped into my office looking for the name and address that the woman gave me yesterday. There it is. Sitting right in front of me. If it was a snake it would have bit me. At least that's what my dad used to say. With the note in hand, I headed to see our sometime appliance repairman. He was making coffee as I came through the door to the shop.

"Hey Sam, two visits in two days, people will talk. What's up?"

"Yesterday, a woman came in shopping for a washer dryer set. When you didn't respond, I tried to sell her a set, but she wanted to talk to you. Funny thing is she couldn't remember your name. I took her name and number. So, here I am." He took the note and read the name.

"How could she not know my name, we lived together for two years. I'm not sure what this is about, but I'll call her and find out. Thanks Sam." I went back to the store to start a new day.

The store was already hopping. Early day customers are looking for new merchandise before anyone could snag it. I walked by the Society Office. Mrs. Dantone popped out and sang out my name, stopping me in my tracks. "Mrs. Dantone, how nice to see you this morning. How are you?"

"Sam, I'm fine, but I don't get down here very much anymore. The Society wants me to visit a family that needs some help. You look good. How's the family?"

"Doing fine. My oldest is ready to graduate. Makes me feel old."

"I know that feeling. See you next time, but I've got to go." She left to make her visit.

I was just getting ready to go to lunch, when the same woman from yesterday walked in.

"May I speak to the manager?"

"I'm the manager, how can I help you?" Linda was very cordial in her response.

"I have a complaint. I spoke to a man yesterday. He promised to give a message to the appliance repairman. I think that he just blew me off."

"Sam, can you come over here?" I smelled trouble as I made my way over.

"That's the man."

"Linda page Doug. Let's go into my office for some privacy."

"Let me introduce myself, I'm Sam Simone, the Executive Director of Stores for the Good Samaritan Society. I don't remember your name."

"I'm Lori Smalls." I waited until Linda returned to start the conversation.

"I paged him, but so far no response."

"Well, let's get started. Ms. Smalls, as to the 'Blowing you off', I gave Doug the message this morning around nine. I resent your accusation, but I can't account for my repairman not calling you as promised. I would hope that Doug has a good reason for not calling."

"I might have spoken more harshly than I intended, but he makes me so angry." There was a knock at my door. Linda opened it. She stepped outside to talk to Bob.

"Bob said that Doug told him that he felt sick and went home."

"May I call you Lori?" Lori nodded. "It seems that this is not about a washer dryer set. I was told by Doug that you and him had a relationship in the past."

"Yes, but we broke up years ago. I lied about not knowing his name. I'm sorry about that. He has made sure that I have never been able to pin him down since the break-up."

"If you're broken-up, why do you need to pin him down?"

"Bossman, she's trying to establish paternity, right?"

"Yes." Came the meek reply. That put a different light on the issue.

"This is all that I'm going to say on the matter. You need to do what you have to, but you can't make a disturbance in the store to do it." I didn't make any promises, but I intended to talk to Doug, if he was ever at work long enough to talk to.

After lunch, I called Doug at home. "Hi Sam. I was expecting your call. I hope that you aren't calling to fire me because I need the job."

"I'm not calling to fire you, but you have to take care of the issue. Angry ex-girlfriends can give the store a bad name. I don't know the circumstances of the paternity thing, so I won't weigh-in on the subject. As for your coming and going as you please, we may have to address that. If your sick stay home, but if you're hiding, get your butt back to work."

"I'll be back in a half-hour. Thanks Sam."

Lori pulled up at her son's school. She wiped her tears away. The doors opened up sending a wave of happy kids out to freedom. Doug was always a straggler. He finally appeared. A big smile spread across her face. The boy was the most precious thing in her life. The worst part of this was that she really didn't know who the father was. When she cheated, her relationship with Doug ended. Ended on bad terms. She didn't know that she was pregnant. The man that she had the affair with laughed at the news. He wasn't going to raise some other guys brat. By then Doug had vanished into thin air. It took five years of looking to locate Doug.

"How was your day, honey?"

"Recess was great. I hit a home run in softball. I didn't do too well on the spelling test. Lunch was pizza."

"That's great, but maybe you should do more studying for the tests."

"Oh, mom." They drove home.

Doug wasn't happy that Lori had found him, but he needed and liked his job. It might just be time to stop hiding and find out if the child was his. Discovering that Lori was having an affair had knocked him for a loop. He thought that everything was alright between him and Lori. He didn't stay around long enough to even ask her why. He grabbed his stuff and hit the road. It was almost a year later when his sister told him that Lori had a baby. From that point he had started moving closer and closer to home. His mind was still fuzzy about the child.

SAM'S OPENING DAY

"Hey, Bossman, is tonight your first softball game?"

"Yeah, at seven-thirty. It is at the Game Farm."

"Josephine asked me to take her."

"That should be fun, I hope that she's been doing well. I haven't stopped by for a while. I mean too, but stuff comes up. I need to be razzed to start the season."

"Are Mac and the rest of your cousins playing?"

"It wouldn't be softball without my cousins. Lately, that is the only time I see them."

"See you tonight." Linda went back to cleaning the store. I on the other hand began daydreaming about softball. The season is neck and neck with soccer. Coaching and playing provide completely different feelings, but I can be myself when I'm playing ball with my cousins and hanging with other players and teams. I love my life, but once in a while I need to grab a bat or a ball and become a kid again. Tonight, would be a good start to the season. The middle game gives me a chance to go home, eat with the family, plus bring a kid or a wife to the game.

"Daddio, you're finally home, guess what?"

"I don't know. Did the chickens come home to roost?"

"No, we don't have any chickens. I get to go to your game."

"That's an outrage, people will hear about this. Does your mom know?"

"She's the one taking me. I can't wait for you to strikeout."

"Just for that, I refuse to strikeout. How about them apples?" My little man began laughing and took off like his pants were on fire. I followed him into the kitchen. He was telling his mom that I was refusing to strikeout for him.

"I see that you've already wound him up. Not home five minutes and now the boy is sad because you refuse to strikeout for him. Just strikeout and make the boy happy. That is my final word."

"Now you have to strikeout. Mom says."

"I love you, both."

We ate a light dinner. I got ready for my game. Jude would show up at game-time with my little fan. If he got tired, Jude would take him home early. I was pretty sure that he would find enough things to do to ward off being tired. The old T-Bird fired right up; as I headed towards my destiny. That better not include any strikeouts.

I unloaded my gear and headed towards a group of my teammates. There are six Simones and Delacs on the team. The rest of the team are old friends from school. We aren't world-beaters, but we have fun, winning enough to keep us coming back.

"How come they keep letting an old bum like you play?" A loud cackle filled the air. Josie was already here and someone bought her candy. I'll get no rest tonight. Linda had brought the oldest living ex-Good Sam employee. Josephine Barrels had worked for Good Sam's until she turned ninety. I had known her since Catholic school. She showed up at my softball games a few times a year and razzed the crap out of me. My teammates called her our lucky charm because we didn't lose many games when she was cackling from the stands. The season felt like it would start on a good note.

Around the third inning, I noticed that the woman, Lori something, was in the stands in the stands. I then realized that Doug was in right field for our opponents. What a weird coincidence. I was on-deck at the time, so I filed it away and got ready for my turn at bat. The game ended after five innings because of the ten-run rule. We left the field happy. Doug wasn't in the after-game line.

"Well, you old bum, I guess that I'll have to watch you play for another season."

"I love you, too, Josie." She hugged the stuffing out of me. Jude came up with David. The little guy looked tuckered out.

"Daddy, you won. I'm glad. I played with all of the kids on the toys."

"Give me a kiss. Thanks for being my fan."

"I better get him home before he keels over. I'll see you at home." I kissed my woman in front of the whole world. The crowd began thinning out. I walked to my car. I heard someone calling my name.

"Sam, may I have a moment of your time?"

"Sure, what can I do for you?" It was that Lori woman.

"I'm not stalking you. Doug called me and invited me to come to his game. I honestly, didn't know that he was playing against your team."

"I never thought that you were stalking me. Maybe, we should start over. My name is Sam Simone."

"Okay, my name is Lori Smalls. Your team had a good game tonight."

"Thank you. This is so much nicer than being angry with each other." Lori relaxed and smiled.

"Sam, I'm hoping that Doug and I can talk. A boy needs a father."

"You're right. I wish you luck." With that we parted. I was ready to head home to my kids. Once again, as I was attempting to get in my car, someone called me, "Sam."

"Hello Mac. What's up?" Mac walked up with an odd look in his eyes.

"That woman you were talking to looks very familiar. I think that we went to school together, but I can't quite remember her name."

"Her name is Lori. I had some business with her at Good Sam's."

"Yeah, Lori, Lori Smalls. I haven't seen her since high school. She looks pretty much the same. It seemed like right after graduation that she disappeared into thin air."

"Did you go to school with Doug, my appliance guy?"

"Yes. He wasn't the friendliest kid in our class. We didn't hang out together, but our paths crossed occasionally. I heard that you'd hired him after Ross retired."

"Good game tonight, Mac. See you on Thursday." I finally escaped to go home.

JOEY GETS ACCEPTED

"Dad, here's the paperwork for the appliance program. I've sent all the college papers in."

"I'll look at them and sign them if everything is correct."

"Great, when the financial aid stuff comes. We can fill them out, too!" Joey ran out the door like a new man.

"Come and eat, before it gets cold." I headed to the kitchen.

"Joey has already filled out all of his college paperwork. He's really on top of this."

"Well, dear, he has a very good reason to want to be on top of this."

"You mean Ginger. I glad that she came into his life. To see him start to grow up and flourish makes me very proud. I worried for a long time that he would just float along until he settled for less than he wanted."

"Are you looking at your teen years?"

"I guess that is part of it, but Joey seemed to put his smarts under a bushel basket. It is nice to see him going for something."

"I agree. Sam you're a good Dad. Have a nice day at work." Jude kissed me and ushered me out the door.

The employee parking area was almost full. The store was a hive of activity. I worked my way around the busy workers making my way to the appliance shop. Doug was busy working on a repair job. "Morning Sam. I didn't know that we were playing your team last night. You guys kicked our butts. Mac Delac is your cousin?"

"One of five on the team. I didn't know that you graduated with Mac."

"We weren't exactly friends. We knew each other and hung around a lot of the same guys, but we weren't close. Mac was a jock. I just was a guy."

"I didn't come in to reminisce. I came to tell you that I have chosen your apprentice for the coming school year. My son is the only applicant, so he'll be starting June 15th. We usually have the classes in the morning, work in the afternoon. The work manuals and class structure are in the locked filing cabinet. All work will be turned into me for approval. Copies will be sent to the college. At the end of the summer, the remaining classes will be at the college. A work schedule will be set up between the student and you. The student will be paid for the hours in training here and the total hours are reported by me to the college. Any questions?"

"No, I take it that Joey has to complete the training manuals and work a predetermined number of hours to complete the training. You will keep track of all his records here and forward them to the school. He is paid for the hours that he works here."

"That's it in a nutshell. This is a good program. We've graduated a dozen people. As far as I know all of them are working in the field."

"Good Sam pays the students. That is great. I wish that I had known about this program when I graduated."

"Oh, by the way, we are planning to start a bike repair program. If we can find a good repair person. Let me know if anyone comes to mind. Thanks for your time, I've got to head back to my office."

"Linda, can you get away for an hour? I'd like to take you to lunch."

"Sure, Bob can take of things for an hour. When do you want to go?"

"Around eleven. I have list of things to go over with you."

"Oh, I see, a working lunch."

"No, a private lunch." We were set for eleven, working or not.

It only seemed like moments when I looked up to see that it was almost eleven. I finished what I was doing and went out to find Linda.

"You're ready? Just let me call Bob to come over." Bob showed up promptly, so we headed to my car. I opened the passenger door for Linda. We headed for a little café on Main Street. They served great soups and sandwiches. No one bothered us when we went there.

After we settled into our booth, the waitress gave us the specials of the day. I didn't need the specials; I always ordered the Hot Pastrami. Linda opted for a cup of soup and a salad. The food was soon devoured.

"I suppose you're wondering what this meeting is all about, well first of all, we need to discuss the bike repair program that I'd like to reinstate. The board didn't want to keep thc program when the bike guy left, but I've always believed that it did a good job of putting decent bikes into low-income family's hands. Finding the right person to fix the bikes is going to be the hard part. I would consider a current employee if they have the skills to put out a good product."

"I'll talk to the employees to see what comes up."

"Did you see who showed up at the game last night?"

"I saw that Doug was playing on the other team, but other than that I had my hands full with Josie." Josie could be a handful when she hadn't been out for a while.

"The woman that came into the store looking for Doug was in the stands."

"Are you sure?"

"I wasn't at first, but after the game she came up to my car. She kind of laughed as she said that she wasn't stalking me. We had a nice conversation about her wanting her son to have a dad."

"Do you think that this is going to turn into a problem?"

"That's the puzzling part, I really don't know. What I'd like you to do is watch out for any out of the ordinary things, also tell Doug that he must report when he's leaving during the day. Have Bob keep track."

"The Doug thing is bugging you."

"I can't read him very well, so this stuff is sending all sorts of weird signals. Better to be safe than sorry. Let's get back to work. Thanks for letting me talk."

"Anytime, Sam."

GRADUATION DAY

The day had finally arrived; Graduation day. Joey had survived all the trials and tribulations of being a kid in today's world. My oldest had been a very quiet, but mischievous child. He wasn't a child anymore. In the last couple of months before graduation, he had displayed a maturity not seen before. The plans he presented to us about school, work, and marriage showed us that he was more ready than I had thought to challenge the world. All of these thoughts were swirling around my head as we were frantically getting ready for the graduation ceremony.

"Daddio, help me get ready for Joey's graduation. Mom's in the shower." David was an energy bomb waiting to go off. He didn't know what a graduation was, but he knew that it was important.

"Okay, little man, I'll help you get ready." We were off to his room to get dressed and groomed.

"Dad, I'll meet you at the graduation. Suzie is coming to get me in her new car."

"Suzie is driving, heaven help us."

"Oh Dad, she's a good driver. Remember that we're in the 'Twelve-year Senior' section."

"We'll be there, don't tell Suzie I made fun of her driving."

"I won't. We'll see you there." I went back to getting David ready. Jude soon appeared. She was absolutely gorgeous. My wife is a vision to me most of the time, today she was beaming. I think that we were ready to go see our oldest pass this big milestone. I took David out to Jude's car.

"Daddy, why does Mom always drive when we go places?"

"Cuz, my car only has two doors, plus Mom doesn't trust my old T-Bird to make it wherever we're going."

"I like your car, even if it's old."

"Thanks David, at least someone besides me likes it." I kissed him as I finished belting him into his booster seat. I opened the door for my lovely wife and we were soon on the road.

Twin Rivers High School was jammed with parents and friends coming together to celebrate this year's graduates. We had to park in the far parking lot and hike to the stadium. The football field was more crowded than the homecoming game. We passed a lot of our old neighbors on the way into the stadium. This was a special night, not only for the students, but for us parents, too! We had got our child to one of the first major hurdles in their lives.

"Sam, do you know where the section is for the 'Twelve Year Seniors'.

"No, but we'll find it or Marie will come guide us to it."

"Little sister seems as excited as Joey. And just think that we get to do this all over again next year." Jude was smiling as she looked over the crowd milling around outside the stadium. I spotted the sign directing parents to the special section. We began working our way through the crowd. Marie spotted us and began waving us towards her. We soon got through the crowd.

"Great, you made it. I have our seats; Suzie is guarding them." We followed our, soon to be a senior, to the seats. After getting us settled in; Marie and Suzie took off for parts unknown.

"I haven't been to a high school graduation since my own. I wonder how long this will be?"

"I'm sure that it will seem longer than it really is. I hope the little guy won't get too bored with all the speeches and ceremonial things."

"Look at him, Sam, he's like a kid at the circus, if anything he'll fall to sleep from exhaustion." She was right.

All three kids were going through their own awe at the graduation. Marie and Suzie returned just as the ceremony was starting.

"There's Joey. See him down on the right. Marie make sure you get some pictures of the different parts of the graduation."

"Don't worry, Mom, between Suzie and I we'll try not to miss anything." The girls were moving around taking pictures. There seemed to be a large group of kids taking pictures.

"Mommy, can I go with Marie to help take pictures?" Jude looked at me. I waved Marie over.

"What do you want?"

"David wants to help you take pictures. What do you think?"

"Sure, I need an assistant. Come on David." David leaped to go with his sister.

"Keep an eye on him. I'll be watching you."

"Oh Dad, of course I'll keep an eye on him. You guys would ground me for life if I lost him." Marie smiled and grabbed her brother's hand.

The rest of the ceremony went off on schedule. Joey was honored for being a Twelve-Year Senior, top five percent in attendance, and being an Honor Roll student.

Joey got up went to school and did the best that he could. As a dad, I couldn't ask for much more. He liked school for the most part, mostly because all of his friends were there and that's where the girls were.

Finally, all the speeches were over. It was time to introduce us to this year's graduates. The school superintendent did the honors, the kids erupted into loud joyous shouts, throwing their caps into the air. Parents and guests gave them a standing ovation, while making their way down to congratulate them.

"Mom, Dad, wasn't it great. Thank you both for being such good parents." Joey was hugging all of us with joy. David ran up to him and got a swing around the stands. He was looking all around.

"Joey, go find her. Have a good time at the party. Don't do anything stupid, but celebrate your accomplishment."

"Thank you, Dad." My son kissed me for the first time since he was ten. I had watery eyes as he left to find his girl. Jude hugged me.

"One down, two to go." We laughed. I grabbed David and the three of us headed to the parking lot.

"Hello, Mr. Simone. You have a good son. I hope that he accomplishes everything that he wants." It was

Superintendent Jacka. I hadn't seen him in nearly two years.

"Thank you, Mr. Jacka. That was a very nice graduation ceremony. It's good to talk to you under these circumstances. We'll be back next year for Marie."

"I hope so, Marie is a large part of the school. We'll miss the Simone kids when their gone."

It took a few minutes to exit the parking lot. Chief Petty's men made it a little smoother than it could have been.

"I think that someone deserves a treat for being so good at the graduation. What do you say, Dad?"

"I think that I was pretty good today, so maybe ice cream for me."

"Daddio, momma means me, not you."

"Okay, so you and I get ice cream, what about mom?"

"Of course, mom gets ice cream, she's always good."

"That's settled. Ice cream for all of us." We all got ice cream and went home. Nobody stayed up very late because it was a work night. I was locking up when Marie showed up.

"Did you and Suzie have a good time?"

"You're not going to believe it, but I think that Suzie has a boyfriend."

"Silly Suzie, our Silly Suzie, wow that is big news. What about you?"

"I haven't found anyone that isn't an immature little boy, yet" Marie gave me a big grin and kissed my cheek.

COMPANY COMES

"Did you have a good time at the graduation party?"

Joey looked a little green around the gills.

"It was fun. I got in pretty late, I'm not sure why I'm still up." I can't believe that he's still upright.

"Just a reminder, you have one week to play before the appliance program starts." I was smiling as I looked at Joey. I remember when I graduated, I may have looked as sorry as he did the next day. I left him in his misery as I headed out the door to work.

There was a store committee meeting this morning at ten. I had time to finish all the morning reports at the store, go over my notes for the meeting and get across town before ten.

School was still in session, so I parked in the back-parking lot. The meeting was in St. Joseph's room. The board members were all there and it looked like we had a few visitors.

"Sam, come over here. I'd like to introduce you to our visitors."

"Be right over, Andy." Andy was talking to a group of people, a couple of men and a couple of women.

"This is Sam Simone, our store director. Sam, this is Robert and Shannon Wells, and this is Pat Jones and Wallace Benning. They are from the national Good Samaritan Society."

"Nice to meet all of you, what brings you to Auburn and Blessed Family?"

"We are surveying groups all across the country to see the types of programs that are available and how different areas implement them." I think that it was Pat or Patricia that answered my question.

"I'd be glad to have you see our programs and show you how we run them."

"That is what we need. Can we talk after the meeting?"

"Sure, I'll help you any way that I can." The meeting was about to start.

Nothing of real importance happened at the meeting. Most of what I brought up was about the store's progress. I had a few items on restarting bike repairing if I could find a qualified repairman. Andy finally adjourned the meeting. Pat and her group moved towards my table.

"Sam, would we be able to come to the store today? We are on a tight schedule."

"I don't have any problems with showing you around today. Come by after lunch. I'll give you what I've got." I said with a smile.

"That's great, another question. My colleagues have lunch plans, but I'm not part of the group that they're meeting, so I was wondering if I could go back to the store with you?" I must have looked a little surprised.

"Yeah, you can ride back to the store with me."

"Are you sure?"

"Yes, I guess that your question caught me a little off guard. Most of the people from the state or regional society offices are a bit aloof."

"That door swings both ways. Everyone is always on their best, most guarded, behavior. We never get to know the people that we meet."

"Well, you're in luck. I am what I am. So, I've been told."

The ride was a little hesitant at first. I didn't quite know how to break the ice. Pat finally mentioned my news making ability. "I have to admit, that when I saw that your stores were on the agenda, I felt like we were going to meet a celebrity."

"I'm not a celebrity. The stories all happened, but not knowing what was said or printed in other places, I can't verify how close to the truth they are."

"Well, there were a few differing versions, but I got the feeling that you'd be an interesting person to talk to." I looked at Pat. She didn't look or feel like Robert Parent or Father Brody. I decided to just take her at face value. I was able to relax and take my guard down.

"The store is up ahead on the right. It's an old building, but we've updated it when we have the money for the projects."

"I have seen worse around the country." Pat seemed to be taking everything in. Mentally gleaming any pertinent information for later use.

"Do you want a tour now, or when the rest of the group arrives?"

"I think that we better wait for the whole group for the big grand tour. Now, if it is okay, I'd like to walk around like a customer. That way I can form my own opinion about your operations."

"That works for me. If you need something, I'll be in my office or at the front counter."

As I worked my way to my office, Linda came up with a quizzical look on her face. "Did you get a donation on the way back from the meeting?"

"Funny, no she is from the national Good Samaritan Society. There are three more coming after lunch to look over our operations. Pat, wasn't involved with what the others were doing at lunch, so she asked for a ride to the store."

"That's good because I don't think Jude would approve of you picking up strange women at work." Linda punched my shoulder as she went back to work. I checked my messages. I had returned most of them when I heard a soft knock on my door.

"Come in." I looked up to Pat coming through the door. "How was your turn around the store?"

"I like the way that you utilize space. You get a lot out of the odd shape of the store."

"Have a seat, thank you, the staff works extra hard to get as much merchandise on the floor as possible."

"If I understand correctly, there are three stores total?"

"Yes, the other two stores are much smaller, but we try to send them a wide variety of items. The managers use a lot of innovation to display their merchandise."

"Can you show us how the warehouse handles the donations?"

"They should be here soon, so let's make our way over to the employee room at the warehouse. I'll have Linda, the manager, bring them over when they arrive." We made our way to warehouse.

"This is the employee breakroom and where we hold store meetings. Can I get you something to drink or snack on?"

"Sure, a cola and some chips." I set down her cola and chips. I sat down across from her with my diet cola.

"May I ask you a personal question?"

"I suppose so." My antenna went up while she took her time asking the question.

"How does your wife handle all of these crazy cases that you've been involved in?"

"All I know is that my wife is a very strong person. She took on a ready-made family that was a mess, we adopted a child that was left with us, and add in the crazy cases as you call them, she is without wavering in her love and support for all of us."

"That's a wonderful tribute. I wish that I could find a strong partner like that."

"I didn't always have a strong partner, but somehow we came together. I thank God every day." Andy and the other guests came into the break room.

The tour and observations took a good part of the afternoon. The questions and observations were intelligent. The group had good insights into the day-to-day workings of a Good Samaritan Store. The last stop on the tour was the appliance repair shop.

Doug was working on a refrigerator. The group crowded around Doug. I started to introduce everyone. When Doug looked at Pat, he turned pale and started to run from the room.

"Doug, don't. I didn't know that you were here." Doug stopped.

"Is there a problem?"

"No, Sam. I just freaked when I saw my ex-wife standing there. We didn't part on good terms."

"Doug and I were married a long time ago. I haven't seen him in six or seven years."

"Maybe, we should head back to my office. We can finish the day with an overview of what you saw and thought, today."

The session ended with a lot of usable information. As the group left, I made my way back to Doug's shop. Doug was finishing the refrigerator he had been working on when the group interrupted him.

"I wasn't expecting another visit. I don't know what I did to have the two women that I screwed up with, both showing up in the same week. Karma has come back to bite me. I'm trying to laugh before I cry."

"I'm not here to pile on, but I need you to do your job as well as you have for the time that you've been here. I know what it's like to have a failed relationship in my past. It makes life hard to handle somedays, but I know that there is light at the end of the tunnel."

TRAINING TIME

I knocked on Joey's door. "I'm up Dad."

"Just making sure, didn't want you to be late on your first day."

"I won't be. I'm taking my car. I have some things to do after the class." I headed to the kitchen for some breakfast. Jude looked up as I came in.

"Is Joey up?"

"Yes. I didn't want him to be late, either."

"Where's David?"

"Still asleep. Marie is watching him today. I have meetings this morning." Jude and I sat down for a quiet breakfast. As we were finishing, Joey appeared and made some toast, before dashing out the door.

"That's my cue. Don't want the kid to beat the boss to work." A peck on my lovely wife's cheek and I was out the door, too!

Pulling into the lot at Good Sam's, I noticed that Joey had beat me to work. With my fingers crossed, I made a small prayer for Joey's success.

The store was alive with employees working to get it ready for the day. I slipped into my office without anyone noticing. Soon, I was engrossed in the morning prep. I checked my calendar for any appointments or meetings that I may have missed or forgotten. I didn't find anything, so I headed out to see how the staff was doing.

"Bossman, you are here. I guess that I'll have to cancel the missing person's report that I called in."

"Good morning to you too, Linda. Anything needed before we let the rampaging herd in?"

"I don't think so, but the rampaging herd called in sick today, so just a few morning regulars will have to do." Linda turned the sign to open. A few regulars straggled in.

"Joey, nice to see you here bright and early. I have your books and some papers to fill out. After the preliminaries, we'll get started on the class. Any questions?"

"I don't think so. I'm kind of excited to get started. I've been reading some stuff on-line about appliances. All of it sounds interesting." The rest of the day was a mix of book work followed by some hands-on experiences. Doug used the actual appliances that he was working on to give Joey some practical applications.

"Well, Joey, two o'clock comes fast when your busy. Take a few minutes to clean your work tools and area. Then, you can get out of here. The work book is yours, so you can take it home to study, but don't forget it. Nice first day."

"Thanks, Doug. I'll see you tomorrow." Joey cleaned his work area, grabbed his stuff and headed out. He was going to Ginger's house. He was so excited that he couldn't wait to tell her how his day had gone.

"Joey looked pretty happy when he left. I wonder how his first day went?"

"I wonder too, but I think that I'll wait till he tells me at home. I'm pretty sure that he's heading to his sweetheart's house to share his day."

"They make such a cute couple. I remember when I couldn't wait to share things with my first major crush."

"Linda, I'll keep you in the loop about Joey."

"I'm curious about how Doug will do as a trainer. The appearance of his two old loves at the same time is really weird. I'm hoping he can keep his mind on work"

"I agree that the timing is weird, but I hope that he doesn't let it interfere with his work. Andy and Al are coming in to discuss the findings of the group that came here. I think that my office will be okay for our meeting."

"I'll send them your way, Sam."

NEW IDEAS

As I reached my office door, I saw Andy, Al, and Pat walk into the store. They headed my way. "If it's alright, we'll use my office for the meeting?"

"That's fine, Sam. Pat wanted to attend to see how we would handle the input."

"Hello, Pat, nice to see you again. Have a seat, everyone."

When we were all seated. Andy handed out folders.

"Take a few moments to look at the information in the folders." I quickly read through the folder. I found nothing very earth-shattering in them. A few tweaks, but nothing outrageous or new. I put the folder down. Andy took that as his place to start.

"As you can see by the suggestions, most of them are just ways of fine tuning what we already do. Sam, I believe that you and Linda should look them over and make recommendations as to which ones will help the store."

"Some of them will work fine, but some will need to be adjusted to fit our programs. I'll have Linda and Bob discuss them and make their recommendations to me."

"Sam, may I be of some help when your people make their revisions?"

"Pat, aren't you going back with the others?"

"No, I've taken a job with the Northwest Region."

"Congratulations, give me your work info and I'll send you a copy of our findings."

"Here is my card. Give me a call anytime you need anything." I don't think in all my years at Good Sam, I've ever needed to contact regional or national people, but you never know. The group got up to depart. I watched them make their way out. Andy hesitated, before turning around.

"Sam, do you have a moment?" We re-entered my office.

"What's up?" Andy looked confused as he searched for an answer.

"Sam, I'm not sure how to start my thoughts. It's about Pat. It seems that she took a temporary position with the regional council. All of this happened after they came to the store. I don't know what it's about. I just know that it has my inner alarm going off."

"I have some inner alarms going off, myself. You do know that she is Doug's ex-wife."

"I knew that it was very awkward when they met. What I don't know is why she made such big decision almost immediately after their meeting."

"It shouldn't be any issue for us. The regional and national people have never spent much time looking at us. Maybe, she has some unfinished business with Doug. Oh, by the way, Doug also reconnected with an old girlfriend this week."

"That doesn't make me feel any better. I hope that these are just coincidences."

After, Andy finally departed, I took a walk around store. I entered the 'Boneyard' when I spotted Old Henry. Henry must have been on his best behavior. No one had come begging me to take care of the old pest.

"Sam, long time no see. Don't worry, I'm being nice today, but as long as you're here, maybe you can give me some prices."

"Sure Henry. Where's Tiny?"

"His daughter took him for a doctor's appointment."

"Is he okay?"

"Yah sure, just a checkup." I gave Henry some prices. We parted amicably. My next stop was the loading dock. Bob and his guys were setting deliveries up for the drivers. No one took any notice of me as I went by them. The sorters were hard at it, as I entered their area. The donation pile was very large. That's always a good sign. I watched as the sorters attacked the huge pile. There was a steady movement of articles to the store ready pile, the second look pile and the waste pile. The ready pile was then broken into groups for the three stores. Auburn's pile was the largest by right of being the largest store. Enumclaw and Covington were sized according the needs of the stores. My last stop would be the appliance shop.

"Where's your trainer, Joey?"

"Hi Dad, he left with some woman about an hour ago."

"What are you doing?" He pointed at his work books.

"I'm working on my lessons. Doug said that he'd be back in an hour."

"Show me what you're working on."

"I'm working on the first three chapters. There is a quiz for each chapter. At the end of the three chapters is a longer test. So far, so good."

"Well, I've got to get back to my office. I'll see you at home."

"Thanks, Dad."

I saw Doug as I was entering the store. He looked guilty as he saw me. He made turn towards my office.

"Did another old girlfriend show up today?"

"No." He said with a sheepish grin. "It was Pat, my ex-wife. She's under the impression that our meeting was some sort of destiny or some other hogwash."

"That explains her transfer. Get back to work."

"What do you mean her transfer?"

"She hasn't told you that she transferred out here?"

"God, what next? I just started to work on the father thing. She could really screw up that." Doug walked away like a broken man.

INTERFERENCE

The next couple of weeks were very quiet, too quiet. Doug was at work every day, all day. I never saw either of his women. Joey was still excited about his training. It was going very smooth, so history had shown me that a storm was coming.

About an hour into Monday, the storm landed. Linda appeared at my door. "Bossman, I think that you should come out here."

"Okay, I'll be right out." As I entered the store, I noticed Pat was leading a man around and pointing things out to him.

"May I help you, Pat?"

"No, I'm just showing the contractor what he needs to do."

"I beg your pardon, but we aren't having any work done. I need to see you in my office. Can you excuse us for a moment?" The man looked startled. Pat followed me into my office.

"I don't know what you're doing, but you need to stop."

"You don't need to know what I'm doing. I'm the regional store director."

"That may be fine, if we were a regional store. We are an independent Good Samaritan store and Society. You can advise us, but you cannot direct us."

"What do you mean that you're an independent store?"

"Call your boss. Ask him what that means. Afterwards tell your contractor that his services are not needed."

"You can't tell me how to do my job."

"Okay, I'll call Jim and he can explain it to you." I called the Regional Director, Jim Connally.

"Hi Sam, what can I do for you today?"

"I need you to explain to Pat Jones how it works with an independent store. Here she is." It was a one-sided conversation. When she handed the phone back to me her face was red, fiery red.

"I'm sorry Sam, she seems obsessed with your operations. She is on loan from the National office, anything else that I can help you with?"

"No, that should do it, thanks." Pat had left the office. I went out to find her and the contractor. The man was patiently waiting in the same spot.

"She went out that side door." I followed in that direction. Bob and Pat were in a very animated conversation.

"Sam, I've explained to her that she couldn't be back here and that no one could come in and demand to look through records."

"You did fine. Pat I'm going to ask you to leave, just one time. If you don't leave, then I'll call 911 to have you removed. Pat, you need to leave."

"How dare you threaten to have me removed. I am a Society representative. I'll have your job over this."

"You just talked to your boss, temporary boss I should say. He explained that we are not under that umbrella. I don't know what your problem is, but you need to pull yourself together and start acting like a professional."

"I'll leave, but you haven't heard the last about this."

"Fine, I'll file it with the rest of the ignorant threats people have hurled at me. Stay out of the store or I'll push it with your boss, capisce." Pat stormed out of the store

An hour later, an Auburn Police car pulled into the parking lot. Two officers got out and walked to the door.

"Good afternoon, officers. How may I help you?"

"It's Sam isn't it?"

"Yes, we met a couple of years ago. What is the problem?" Officer Wetzl and I met the night David came into our lives.

"Can we go someplace private?"

"Sure, my office is right over there." The three of us made our way to the privacy of my office.

"I have a feeling that you already know what this is about, so here goes. A complaint has been filed against you by a woman named Pat Jones. She alleges that you illegally barred her from performing her duties and aggressively threw her out of the store."

"Pat Jones is not an employee of the Good Samaritan Stores of South King County. She appeared without notice with a contractor to start some type of construction project. I tried to talk to her about this, but she wouldn't take no for an answer. I called her boss, Jim Connally of the Regional Good Samaritan Society. He informed her that she had no jurisdiction over our stores. I asked her to leave, but she stormed out of my office. I found her in our warehouse area arguing with Bob, the assistant manager. At that point I asked her to leave. I told her that if she didn't remove herself and her contractor, I would call 911. She left spewing threats all the way out the door. That was about an hour ago."

"Her story claims that you made up the part about her not having jurisdiction over these stores. She claims that your body language was threatening to her. Do you have any witnesses to the confrontation?"

"Like I said, Bob the assistant manager and the other workers in the sorting area. I have Jim Connally's phone number to verify my and Pat's conversation with him." Bob and his crew were soon in my office answering questions. Officer Wetzl had a nice talk with Jim Connally verifying what I had reported."

"Mr. Simone, I think that we have enough. Let us know if Ms. Jones comes back. It has been a pleasure to meet you."

"Call me Sam, I didn't catch your name."

"Sgt. Dargey." We shook hands. The officers headed back out to their car.

"Sam, what is with that woman?"

"I don't know, but she went from very pleasant to pyscho as soon as she saw Doug. I have to call Jim Connally back. I'll talk to you after the call." I took a moment to catch my breath.

"Good Samaritan Regional Society, how can I direct your call?"

"I'd like to talk to Jim Connally."

"This is Jim, what can I help you with, today?"

"Jim, Sam Simone, we need to talk about my little problem. Do you have a moment?"

"I always have a moment for you. I think that I've solved the problem. As of ten minutes ago, Pat Jones is no longer employed by the Society. I hope that stops whatever it is that sent her off the deep end."

"Thanks, Jim, but inside it feels like it might just be the start. I know that you're busy so I'll let you go."

AN UNEASY PEACE

Nothing out of the ordinary happened for a week. That came to a crash when Doug was leaving work on Friday afternoon. His car had been vandalized. All four tires were flat and the vandal wrote a few nasty notes on the car. I called Auburn's finest to report the incident. It just so happened that Wetzl and Dargey came on the call.

I was outside with Doug as they pulled up. Doug was taking pictures of the damage with his phone.

"Afternoon, Sam. Where is the owner?"

"I am officer. My name is Doug Toms."

"How long was it parked out here?"

"I pulled in at nine this morning. I didn't come back until four." Sgt. Dargey took Doug aside to take his statement.

"Sam, do you think that this has anything to do with his ex-wife?" Wetzl asked as he came towards me.

"It could, she was very angry. I don't know their background, but from my experience with her, it is possible."

"She has been calling the station daily since she got shot down. There is nothing in our local records about her. She hasn't done anything to justify us looking into outside records. If there was a way to see her background records it might save us some grief later." Officer Wetzl was hinting very loudly that I should look into her background.

"If I knew a way to look, I would do it. I guess that I can ask around. If something comes up, do you have a card?"

"Sure Sam, let me know if you find anything." I headed back into the store. I was curious what my friend would find.

"Sam, nice to hear from you. What's up?"

"I have a job for you. The subject's name is Patricia Jones. She was employed by The Good Samaritan Society's national office. Ex-husband's name Doug Toms. I'm not sure what we need or what's in the records, just dig. Let me know as soon as you have something on her. She is becoming a pest."

"I'll jump right on it. It's been kind of slow lately. I was starting to rust."

"We can't have that happening. Regular rates. Thanks Fatty."

I felt a little better with Fatty looking into Ms. Jones.

Joey stopped my office as he was leaving. "Dad, what happened to Doug's car?"

"Someone flattened all of his tires and wrote crap all over his car."

"I hope they find who did it. Doug seems a little off since his exes showed up. What a mess. I won't be home for dinner. Ginger and I are going out to eat. See you later."

"Okay, have fun." I went back to my reports. I found a strange message from the Good Samaritan office. I checked the time to see if they'd still be there. They had another hour before closing.

"Good Samaritan Society, how can I help you?"

May I speak to Jim Connally, please?" Jim soon answered.

"Jim Connally, how can I help you?"

"This is Sam the pest. I got a strange message from your office about a bill for services."

"What does the message say?"

"It says that this invoice is being forwarded to the South King County Good Samaritan Stores for services. It is signed by Director of Stores, but no name is attached."

"Does it have a vendor name?"

"Yes, I'm sorry. The vendor is Value Construction."

"That is the contractor that was with Pat Jones last week. I will have a word with them. Send the invoice back to us. I think that is another shot from Ms. Jones. I'll fix this, but it may not be the last word from my ex-employee. Keep in touch." The weird day came to an end. I drove home with thoughts of what might be coming next.

"Jude are you home?"

"I'm out back with David." Out back is where I headed. David was putting on a performance for his Mom. The boy was running, jumping, and enjoying life as only a child can. He spotted me, making a beeline towards me. As he leaped, he yelled, "Daddio!" His greetings are out of this world. We ended in a heap of giggling, smiling, joy.

"What do they feed him?"

"He's been this way since I picked him up."

The welcome home greeting had taken my mind off of employees' crazy ex-wives. David went back to running and jumping, Jude and I headed into the house.

"I have a game tonight at eight, I'm not sure if I reminded you."

"You didn't, but I checked the schedule. I don't think that we're going to go. David is wound up enough without a late game to throw him off even more."

"I didn't think that you were going. There will be other games and other nights."

"Joey told me that he was doing something with Ginger. It's weird, someone vandalized Doug's car. The police are assuming it was his ex-wife. The officer told me that she has been calling the department every day."

"There is a big hole in Doug's story, but it seems that his ex is a little bit off. I hope that we're not going down the rabbit hole."

"I have nothing to do with Doug's love life. I am hopefully retired from finding bad things." We both laughed.

I got to my game a little early. Grabbing my gear, I headed to the stands to watch last part of the early game. I enjoy watching a few innings of softball every once in a while. As I settled in, I noticed the woman sitting a few feet over. Lori Smalls was looking very relaxed as she watched the game. She turned towards me as I sat down.

"Hi again, how are you tonight?"

"I'm fine, Lori, you're becoming a fan of softball."

"I guess that you might say that. I can soak up some sun, Doug can play with the other kids on the toys, and I like watching the guys play. I feel a little less lonely. Where's your family, tonight?"

"The late games throw David, my youngest, off his routine. He was full of it when I came home from work."

"I know the feeling, sometimes mine doesn't wind down until he wakes up the next morning." We both laughed. We talked for a few more moments until my teammates showed up and I had to go warmup. We won a boring game. I noticed that Lori left not too long after our game started. Driving home, I was happy about my game, I got three hits, but something was nagging me about Lori. She was not a happy person.

A NEW CAR FOR DOUG

Pulling into Good Sam's there was a crowd gathered around a car in the employee parking area. I got out and decided to check out the scene. I spotted Doug leaning against a fairly new Dodge Challenger. The crew was giving the car an inspection, oohing and drooling all over it. I have to admit that it was a good-looking machine, but I wouldn't trade my old T-Bird for it.

"Nice car, Doug. What did you do with the old one?"

"Put it in the garage until I repaint it."

"All right, everybody, we've got a store to open." The looky-loos headed in to start the day.

I was scheduled to visit our other stores today. My plan was to get as much done as I could, before heading out. Linda and I tried to visit each store at least once a month. If there were any problems, we may have to go even more often. Linda had most of the store and warehouse crew cleaning the store. She wanted to make sure that everything was ahead of schedule before we left.

"Did you bring everything for the road trip?"

"I'm not listening to Steppenwolf this time. We can talk about store matters instead of listening to old rock and roll."

"You're no fun, but I see that you have a solid hand on the store. I'll be ready about ten. Could you send Bob to my office, please."

"Sure, Bossman."

When Bob showed up, I gave him some last-minute instructions. Linda and I were in the T-bird ready to go at ten. We headed for Covington first, so I took the onramp for eastbound 18. It wasn't long before we approached the exit to Kent-Kangley Road. Denise had an appointment this afternoon, so that's why we started with the Covington store.

Denise was helping a customer when we walked in. The store had been rearranged since out last visit. This is one of the attractions of this store. Denise rearranged and reimagined the layout on a regular basis. I have received a lot of complimentary calls about how much customers liked the changes and surprises when they walked into the store. Denise was finally finished helping her costumer. She smiled and headed towards us.

"It's nice to see you guys. I hope the drive was uneventful. Let's take a walk around as we talk."

"The store is looking good, but it always does."

"Thanks, Sam." Linda had made her way to a display in the back of the store.

"Denise, I like this display, can I steal the idea for Auburn?"

"Be my guest, I get a lot of comments about it." Linda had her phone out taking pictures of the display. We toured the rest of the store. It wasn't a long visit. Denise always keeps the store immaculate. The only problem that I've ever had with the Covington store was that it wasn't big enough, but the board couldn't afford anything larger. Now I wouldn't change it. We said our goodbyes. And we were on the road to Enumclaw.

"Sam, you know that if we ever lost Denise that store wouldn't be the same."

"I know, but that's why we need to be creative with our employees. Keeping the good ones, plus finding the gems, when we needed replacements. I honestly, didn't see what a creative person Denise was, until she took over the store."

"I have a couple of gems in the store, Angela and Amy. Those two are ready for bigger and better things, I just hope we can keep them."

"I've always thought that Angela was a keeper. Wasn't Amy the sorter with the polyester problem?"

"Yes, from the day that you took a few moments to give her some advice and attention, she has become my best sorter. She can fill in at just about every position."

"That's good to hear. If it's alright with you, I think that we'll eat after the store visit."

"Sure, Bossman, as long as you feed me."

It took a little time to find parking in Enumclaw. Linda and I had to walk a block to the store. Amanda and Jenny must have posted lookouts. They greeted us like our ship had just docked.

"Sam, Linda, so nice to see you. Come in, come in." It was a little overboard, but I sometimes liked being buttered up. I hope it was for a positive reason.

"Nice to see both of you, too!"

"Impressive, the store looks busy." Linda added.

"Can we talk in my office for a moment?"

"Lead the way." Amanda, Linda, and I headed to the office. Jenny stayed to watch the store. Amanda's office was small. Not much room for amenities.

"I suppose that you're wondering why I need to talk to you? I just found out that my husband is being transferred. I have to give my notice. We'll be moving in a month." The look on Amanda's face wasn't happy or sad, just blindsided. I know that all of her family lived in the Enumclaw area.

"That is certainly, not what I was expecting. I hope it is a good thing for your family. I, as a person and your boss, will miss you. I have one question, is Jenny ready to take your place?"

"That is one of the problems, Jenny is ready, but she can't take on more hours because of her children and her parents. She takes care of her parents"

"Is Jenny willing to continue in her current position?" Linda asked.

"Yes, as far as I know, but ask her."

"You have done such a good job. The store was failing when you replaced Betty. This store is in great financial shape, now."

"Thank you, Sam. I'll go get Jenny." Amanda left to fetch Jenny. Jenny appeared and sat down.

"Jenny, it looks like some big changes are coming to the store. First thing is, are you interested in the manager's job?"

"Yes, I would be, but I can't add any more hours to my day. So, no is my answer."

"Okay, my second question, do you want to stay in your current position?"

"Yes, I certainly would. Do you have any idea about Amanda's replacement?"

"Well, Linda and I have to discuss this. Before making a decision about whether we have anyone in house, or if we'll have to hire from the outside. It would have been an easy decision if you could have taken the job, but when a choice is made, I will talk to you again."

We left after assuring both of them that we would be back after making a decision. Not much was said on the drive back to Auburn. We were headed to The Main Street Café for lunch. There would be plenty of time to talk at lunch.

The staff promptly showed us to a nice clean booth. We took a few minutes looking at their large menu of American diner classics. This place specialized in comfort food, served in good sized helpings. Sometimes, I had to loosen the belt buckle after one of their meals. I ordered the daily special, roast beef with mashed potatoes and gravy. Linda ordered a chef's salad. The food arrived shortly. I made fast work of mine. Linda finished soon after.

"Do you have anyone ready to take on the job at Enumclaw?"

"I think that Angela or Amy are quite capable of doing the job. Angela has more time and experience, but Amy once she connected with what we wanted, learned at a faster pace."

"We'll interview them tomorrow morning. Depending on what they say, we'll try to choose a replacement. I also think that Jenny needs to be bumped a little in pay. She will be handling a lot of the daily training, plus she needs to feel that we want to keep her."

"I think that's a good idea. A happy Jenny will make this an easier transition. Let me ask you a question about Doug. Do you feel that the problems of the last few week are going to get worse?"

"I've been mulling that over. I don't have an answer yet."

"By the way, Bob may have found a bike guy. I'll ask him again, when we get back."

"That's good, if it works out, we can take one more thing off of our to-do list. I'll pay the bill, but that means we have to go back to work."

"Joey, I want you to take the apart this dryer. When you have it apart, inspect all of the electrical parts."

Joey started his task. He carefully took the machine apart, placing each part on the work bench. When the dryer was disassembled, he began inspecting the parts. As he inspected, he found two parts that were defective. He set them to the side, before finishing his inspection.

"Well, let's see how you did." Doug looked the parts over. He retested all of the electrical parts. Nothing was said as he examined the dryer. "I must say that I'm impressed. You found the faulty parts. Now, I want you to replace the bad parts and rebuild the dryer. When you rebuild it, replace the belt too!"

Joey worked on the dryer for nearly an hour. Doug was busy on some customer repairs when Joey tapped him on the shoulder. "I'm finished. Check out my work."

Doug looked at the dryer before plugging the pigtail in. "Turn it on and let's see how you did." The dryer sprang to life as Joey turned the knob. A sigh of relief escaped Joey.

"Nice job, now clean it till it shines. You have your first appliance ready for the store." Doug slapped Joey on the back. Joey felt elated that he'd accomplished the task. He cleaned the dryer as fast as he could. Doug took some pictures as he worked. When the dryer was done, Doug applied the warranty and Good Sam's price tag. Joey grabbed the hand truck. The two men wheeled the appliance into the store.

"Attention everyone, I'm Doug the appliance guy, this is Joey my apprentice. I'd like everybody to give Joey a big hand. This dryer is the first machine that Joey has diagnosed and repaired. Let's give Joey a big hand." The customers and employees gave Joey a cheer. I came out of my office when I heard the announcement catching the tail end of Joey's acknowledgment. I was having a proud papa moment.

"Is that a smile on your face, Bossman?"

"Yes, I admit that seeing my kids have some success brings a smile to my face. Look, I think that it has already been sold." Sure enough, the dryer was being purchased by an older couple.

"Bossman, do you have a minute?" Linda asked.

"What's up?"

"I talked to Bob about the bikes. He wants to take stab at the job. I told him to talk to you."

"That's great, I'll wait for him to ask me."

MARIE LEARNS TO DRIVE

Marie was standing in the front yard as I drove up. She didn't seem to be doing anything, just standing. As I got out of the car, she turned towards me. "Dad can I ask you a favor?"

"Sure, honey, what is it?"

"Would you take me for a drive? I just got my permit."

"How did you get your permit?"

"On-line. Now I need to get to the DMV before it closes."

"Is Jude Home?"

"Not yet, that's why you have to take me. We have time to get there and finish the process."

"Get in." I must have missed some days or something. I was sure that we had more time before Marie would be driving, oh well. I should have seen it coming when she said that Suzie had a car.

"Don't worry, I have everything that I need to get my permit. I also signed up for driver's training. It starts in a week." How could I not worry? Marie was a smart, headstrong woman-child. She would be telling the driver's instructors how to drive before the training was over.

At the DMV, we headed in finding that it wasn't very crowded. That was a surprise, I remember when the line would go out the door. Marie found the correct line and we waited a short time for her turn.

"Your permit copy and papers, please." The clerk looked over the papers, stamping each as needed.

"That will be twenty-five dollars." I paid the amount. The clerk gave me a receipt, before motioning Marie to the photo line. A photo was taken of my beaming daughter. The clerk gave Marie her temporary permit. We were in and out in less than fifteen minutes.

"Do you want to drive home?" A giggle escaped my daughter.

"Really, you're going to let me drive the T-Bird?"

"How else are you going to drive us home?"

"Yes, thanks Dad."

She hopped in and started adjusting the seat and mirrors. I went over a few points before she started the car. I was nervous, but I suspected that her and Suzie had been practicing for this moment. Marie made her way out of the lot into traffic. She was being very careful. We went about ten miles under the speed limit. I watched her like a hawk, a nervous hawk. With a sigh of relief Marie turned into our driveway. She had done a very good job on her first father-daughter drive. I must say that I did better with her, compared to my first time with Joey.

We had an audience when we got out of the car. Jude and David came out to meet us. "Well, what have we here?"

"You're looking at the latest member of the Simone family to be almost legal to drive."

"You got your permit, that's great." Jude gave Marie a big hug.

"Daddio, how did you survive the first trip?"

"Just fine, she did a good job, but I'll need all those years to get ready for you, little man."

The Simones all headed inside. Marie went off to tell Suzie about her accomplishment.

"You know that we should look for a safe car for Marie?"

"I know. I'll try to keep an eye out for something that will please her and not break the bank."

"That might be hard. Do you have any idea about what kinds of cars she might like?"

"No, but I might bring the subject up at dinner."

"I wonder if the kids know what a good dad you are?"

"Deep down, I think they know that we're good parents. I just want her to be safe out on the streets. By the way, what are we doing for dinner?"

"I heard that you're ordering teriyaki."

"I think that's very nice of me. I don't know if Joey will be joining us. He had a very exciting day. Repaired his first appliance and it sold as soon as it hit the floor. Doug made a little announcement when they brought the dryer into the store. A couple bought it as soon as Doug was done with his announcement."

"I hope that Joey is really learning something from this program. Learning a craft while going to school. That's a good deal."

"All that I can say is so far, so good."

As we were enjoying our teriyaki, Marie was fidgeting very noticeably. "Something wrong, Marie?"

"No, not really, but I was thinking about what type of car that I wanted."

"What type of cars do you like?"

"Get her a fast one, Daddio." David had to add to the issue.

"No, David, we're not getting her a fast one. A safe one, but not a race car."

"Mom, you're no fun." Two very different children answered at the same time.

"I'm your mom, not the fun zone."

"Marie, mom and I just started talking about it, so if you can tell us what you might like and if it fit your needs, we'll try to find something."

"That's great, thank you both. You are both the best."

Dinner was over. Jude and I cleaned up the mess. David went to play in his room. Marie was still spreading the news of her permit to the masses.

Joey came in around nine. He stopped to chat about his day. "Dad, can you believe it, I repaired and sold an appliance. So far, this class has been more than I thought it would be."

"I came out just in time for Doug's speech. I have to tell you that was one of the fastest appliance sales I've ever seen, good job. By the way, Marie got her permit today."

"That's cool, what type of car are you getting her?"

"Mom and I are still looking into that."

"Doug told me that he was going to sell his old car. It just needs tires and a paint job. He said nothing else was damaged."

"I'll keep that in mind." Joey went off to work out in the garage.

THE END OF SUMMER

The end of summer seemed to be closing in way too fast. Marie was starting practice for her senior year of soccer. David would be starting kindergarten. Joey was scheduled to combine the appliance class with a full college schedule. Needless to say, we were one busy family. School shopping combined with work, driver's ed, preseason practice, and everything else that goes along with having children, kept us on our toes.

Marie's fall practice ended before I got off work. Joey picked her up when he could. Sometimes she headed to Suzie's till I could pick her up. Maybe, getting her license and a car wasn't a bad idea. Joey wasn't going to be there to get her, plus David was starting all-day kindergarten in a week.

I was working on some monthly records when I heard a knock on my door. Putting my papers aside, I opened the door. "Doug, come on in. How can I help you?"

"Sam, I was wondering if you were still in the market for a car?"

"You must have been reading my mind. Tell me about your car."

"It's a five-year-old Elantra. Since it was damaged, I have started it every couple of days, but haven't done anything about the tires or the paint. You can have the car for a thousand, with you replacing the tires and painting it."

"Let me see how much a five-year-old Elantra goes for."

Looking on-line, I soon saw that it was a pretty good deal. Doug and I talked about getting the car checked over by a mechanic. We made arrangements to get it to the garage that worked on the Good Sam trucks. Doug looked happy and I hoped Marie would be happy. The garage that we used had over time become my own personal garage. The owner sent me a quote on tires and painting. The total deal would still come in under the average value of this car. I guess that if it checks out mechanically, I'll make the deal.

Marie had news when she came home from practice.

"You're not going to believe it, but Coach Cummings is out. I don't know why, but the new coach will be here tomorrow. I'm nervous. I didn't like Cummings, but we had the first winning season in school history last year. We, I mean the seniors were hoping to go out on top. I guess that I'll just keep my fingers-crossed. We have talent."

"That is a shock. You guys will be fine. Relax, and meet the new coach before you go off the deep end. You girls have won at every level, so why should this be any different?"

"You're right, Dad. It just seems that everything is coming at different angles this year."

"Just do your best." I gave Marie a hug.

"Morning, David. How are you this morning?"

"Daddy, I've been thinking. How comes I have to go to school? I should be able to wait until I want to go to school."

"Wait a minute, you don't want to go to school or just not now?"

"I don't know. I have friends at the pre-school and I'm not sure if I'll have any friends in school. If I don't have any friends there, then I don't want to go."

"That is a good point, but you'll make new friends at school. Every one of us had to go to school. We all had to try and make friends. School will teach you a lot of important stuff that you'll need for when you get bigger. I will promise you one thing, that Mom and I will always be your friends."

"Okay, Daddio, I'll go." David went back to eating his breakfast. I hope it will always be that easy to solve a problem for David. I know that it won't.

"Jude has Marie left for school, yet?"

"Suzie picked her up a few minutes ago."

"I'm going to look at a car today."

"Is it very old?"

"No, it's a five-year-old Elantra. If it looks okay, I think that I'll get it for Marie."

"That will be another thing off of our back to school list."

I had to finish a few items at work, before getting a chance to talk with Doug. On my way over to the warehouse, I spotted Lori Smalls, Doug's old girlfriend.

"How are you today, Lori?" She looked up with a very pleasant smile as she responded.

"I'm very well, thanks for asking. You know, I've lived in Auburn my whole life, but until I came in to talk to Doug, I'd never stepped foot in here. I think that I'm becoming a regular."

"That's my plan, get a customer in the door and they'll come back again and again. Are you looking for anything in particular or just shopping?"

"Just shopping, I have a long morning break at work, so here I am."

"Glad to see you." I continued on my way to speak to Doug.

Doug and Joey were working on a refrigerator when I walked in. I watched for a moment before they noticed me.

"What brings you our way this morning?"

"I think that I'd like you to go ahead with what we talked about yesterday. If all goes well, it will be ready by the time that I need it."

"That's great, Dad. I hope that she appreciates it as much as I did. In case that I never told you, I do appreciate it."

"I knew. You never wrecked it or ran up a huge amount of speeding tickets. We'll see if your sister is as careful as you with her driving."

"I wouldn't bet the farm on that, not with her competitive juices."

"So, Doug, is there anything that the appliance department needs?"

"Yes, there is, but I was putting together a formal want sheet. It's almost ready."

"Give it to me when you're done. I just ran into Lori in the store. It was a very nice encounter compared to our first

one. You guys have a good day." I headed back to the
office.

"Your Dad is a good guy and a good boss, too! I have
some weird feelings about my exes. I hope it doesn't cause
anyone else problems." Joey and Doug went back to work.

SAM BUYS A CAR, GETS A STALKER

I was supposed to meet Doug at the Auto Service Center at 5:30. Linda and Bob had everything handled at the store, so I told them that I was heading over to get a look at the car.

I looked but didn't see Doug's new car. However, I did notice a woman sitting in a familiar car in the lot, Lori Smalls. I headed in to find Bill Johnson the manager of the Auto Service Center.

"Is Bill in?"

"He's in the back. Look for an Elantra." I went towards the back of the shop. There was Doug's graffiti mobile. Bill was busy checking the car over. Doug walked up before Bill noticed us.

"I didn't see you guys, but I can tell you that this car has been well taken care of." We walked around the car as Bill pointed out what was needed to make it a nice little car.

"After tires and paint, I'd do an oil change. Brakes looked good, everything that I've checked, so far, is in pretty fair shape." Bill looked, waiting for us to say something.

"Alright, go ahead with the tires, paint, and service. I trust you with our trucks, so I'll trust you with this one. Okay, let's do it." Doug was silent through most of the inspection.

"Let me know what color you want and we'll get started."

"Midnight blue for the color and the same grade tires that I put on my cars."

"Sam, how do you want to handle this?" Doug asked.

"Have you put anything out of your pocket?"

"No."

"Then I'll give you a check or cash, depending on what you want. The shop will bill me for all of the work."

"A check is fine. I'll write you a bill of sale and release my interest in the vehicle." As we reached the front counter, I stopped to give my information to the shop for the rest of the work.

"Thanks, Doug, I hope it makes my daughter happy."

"It will, that's a nice little car. I might even have missed it if I hadn't bought the Dodge."

"By the way, as I was coming in, I noticed Lori in the parking lot."

"She and Pat are an odd mixture. Pat sends messages every day, Lori has been very quiet for a couple of weeks. I still don't know what to make of them."

"All I know is that I've seen Lori a number of times in the last few weeks."

"Bill, can you set up the invoices to be billed to me. I'm going to buy the car. It's for my daughter. The things you do for love." We both laughed. Bill had four children, so he has gone through all the same things.

I had to stop at the grocery store on my way home. My list had just a few essentials on it, because it was just a mid-week stop. As I browsed the isles, I began getting a feeling like someone was behind me. I came out of an isle and ran into Lori Smalls.

"Sam, funny meeting you here."

"Lori, nice to see you again. I didn't know that you shopped here."

"I follow the sales. When you're a single mom, shopping for good deals is essential. I like to see a man taking care of everyday things like shopping. I bet that you help around the house, too!"

"Every one, pitches in at my house. If you want to eat or have clean clothes, you need to help."

"I better let you go. I could keep talking forever. See you."

I wasn't sure what had just happened, but it troubled me for some reason. I've never been very good at reading a woman's signals. I may be just overreacting, but I seem to be running into Doug's ex-girlfriend a lot. I hope that they're just coincidences, but my smell meter is going crazy. At least Lori seems normal. If it was Pat, I might be a little more worried.

I hauled my purchases into the kitchen. It seemed, that I was the only one home. The groceries were put away and I'd poured myself a diet cola, when I noticed the land-line was flashing. We might be one of the last holdouts with a house phone, but a lot of messages get captured on it. I pushed the play button. "Sam, we're running late be home by 6:30. Love you."

That explained the empty house. I started dinner. The smell of chicken soon filled the room. Chicken breasts and rice. Simple and filling. I was sitting at the kitchen table relaxing when I heard a car pull up. I looked out the front window just in time to see Lori Smalls pulling out of the driveway. I was starting to get angry. What could she want? Before my anger could overwhelm me, another car pulled in. It was Jude. My anger started to recede. David ran into the kitchen, smiling his biggest smile for me. Jude came in right after him. I was almost back to normal.

"Are you okay?"

"I am now. After we eat, I'll tell you about it." We sat down to a nice quiet meal. The older kids showed up as we finished.

"Grab some plates. Dinner is in the oven. What do you want to drink?"

"Milk for me, Dad."

"I'll grab a coke from the refrigerator."

"This is good, Dad. I was starving at practice."

"So how was the first practice with the new coach?"

"It went very well. The coach is a new teacher at the school. He used to be the head coach at Elma, other than his name, which is Mickey Jones, that's all I know."

"Just be you and you'll be fine. Clean up after you're through."

"Okay, Dad." I went to find Jude. Her and David were relaxing in the family room. David was playing with cars on the floor. Jude was channel surfing.

"What was it that you were going to tell me?"

"Well, I think that I have a problem developing with Doug's ex-girlfriend. I have accidently run into her almost every day over the last few weeks. Today, she was parked at the garage when I went to check over the thing we talked about. Just a couple of minutes before you got home tonight, she pulled into our driveway and drove away."

"Was it a little green car?"

"Yes."

"I had to wait for her to move out of the driveway before I could pull in." Jude paused before continuing. "Are you sure that it isn't just coincidences?"

"That's the problem. They could be nothing, but my smell meter is going crazy. I just don't have any idea why."

"I'm sorry, but I can't give you any advice right now. When you run into her, is she friendly, or is she flirting?"

"I honestly don't know. You know that I'm terrible at reading signals. I just don't know."

"I wouldn't worry too much. It's probably just an infatuation. It'll go away in time." We dropped the subject for now. Jude found an old movie to watch. I was soon snoring.

SAM GETS IRRITATED

I think that I might be losing my mind. I have run into Lori Smalls at least twice every day for the last week. She is always friendly with a smile. She never says anything outside of small talk. You know, how's the weather, nice day, I love the stuff in your store. Lots of people pass my way every day, but it seems that wherever I am, I look up and see Lori. It would be much easier to figure out if she was wacky or nasty, but she is a nice enough person that might be a friend if she wasn't driving me to distraction.

Linda and I were trying to put up a display idea that we got from Denise in Covington. It took a couple of tries before it went into place. We took a step back to admire our work. A voice interrupted us.

"That looks very nice." I turned to see Lori standing next to us.

"Lori, we have to stop meeting like this." Lori's face turned red and she marched out of the store.

"What was that about, Bossman?"

"Your guess is as good as mine. That reminds me we need to interview our candidates for the Enumclaw job."

"Your office or the breakroom?"

"My office." Linda went to get Angela and Amy. I retreated to the safety of my office.

Linda poked her head in my door. "Which one first?"

"Angela." Linda and Angela came in and sat down.

"Good morning, Angela. I suppose that you're wondering why we asked you here this morning."

"Yes, since there's been no gossip lately, I'm curious."

"Here goes, there is a job opening that we think that you're qualified for, so we want to discuss it with you and our other candidate." Angela wasn't showing any reaction as we started. "The Enumclaw store has an opening for a manager. This is a full-time position at a much higher pay scale. Linda and I believe that you are our most qualified employee. Are you interested in this position?"

"Certainly, I'm interested, but I'm not sure about adding the extra commute to my day. I really like my job and am interested in advancing. I'm just not sure of the timing."

"Thank you for your honesty. After we're done interviewing, we will follow up with each candidate before making a decision." Angela left and Amy came in. Amy seemed perplexed as she sat down.

"Amy, we asked you to come in because we have a job opening and you are one of our in-store candidates. Linda and I are very impressed with your ability to learn new tasks. We feel that you are ready to handle this new position. We are looking for a manager to take over the Enumclaw store."

"Wow, I never thought that I'd have much of a chance to move up. This is something that I've thought of a lot. I live closer to Enumclaw. I, also have a two-year degree in business management."

"How come you didn't put that on your application?"

"I completed it while working here."

"Thank you, Linda and I will discuss what we've heard today from both of our candidates. We will follow up with both of you, when we make our decision. Thanks, Amy." After both interviews were over, I turned to talk to Linda.

"I'd like your thoughts on the interviews." Linda paused before starting her answer.

"I think that both are very good candidates, but in my opinion, Amy is our only choice based on her qualifications and answers. She may have more upside."

"I agree with you, Amy is the one that I'd pick for the job, too!"

"Maybe, we could name Angela head cashier, giving her a small raise."

"That is a very good idea. I think that we'll announce our decision in the morning, after we sleep on it."

"Bossman, I don't think that we'll change our minds."

"I know, but a little suspense doesn't hurt. Right now, I need to get something from my car." I wasn't sure why I had an overwhelming urge to go out to my car. As I approached my car, I saw a paper in my windshield wipers.

It said, "Sam, I can't believe that you spoke to me the way you did. Our relationship was moving along very smoothly. I know that you are the one for me. My heart is aching right now. Your Love."

I tried to get the note out of my hand. What in the world is going on? I quickly looked my car over. I didn't see any damage. Slowly, I turned and headed back into the store. Linda saw me walking in holding the paper in my hand.

"What's that Sam?" I held out my hand.

"Read it." Linda took the note and read it.

"Whoa, that's creepy. What are you going to do?"

"I don't know, but I'm going to talk to her ex, Doug."

I decided that it would be more private and official if I called Doug to my office. I asked Linda to be a witness, so nothing could come back at me. Doug soon arrived at my office.

"Come in and have seat. If you don't mind, Linda is going to sit in on our meeting."

"I don't mind, I'm just wondering what's going on."

"That's fair enough. I would like to talk to you about Lori. Please look at this this." I gave the note from my car to him.

"I don't know what to say about this. I do know that it is her writing. I used to get lots of notes like this when we dated. I'll tell you this, she told me yesterday, that she didn't want to see me anymore. I asked her why, but she wouldn't give me a reason. I would venture a guess that the note is the reason."

"Has Lori asked you questions about me?"

"No, the only thing that she's ever said to me was that you were a nice guy."

"Thanks, Doug. I'm just trying to figure out how to handle the situation. Go on back to work." Doug stepped out. Linda looked at me with a funny look on her face.

"Sam, Lori is a very damaged person. I don't think that you can predict how or what she is going to do next."

"I have to agree with you, but she seems so normal when I talk to her."

"Maybe, you should talk to the police. At least get it down that she is, at the least, stalking you. It might help."

"I'll call one of the officers that came about the Pat problem." Linda went back out to bravely face the throng of customers in the store. I found Sgt. Dargey's card and called him.

"Sgt. Dargey, Auburn Police Department, how can I help you?"

"Sergeant, this is Sam Simone, do you have a minute?"

"Sure Sam, what can I help you with today?"

"The other day when you investigated the car vandalizing, Doug, the car owner, was sure it was his ex-wife Pat Jones, but in the same time-frame that Pat has been around, Doug's ex high school girlfriend has appeared and caused a fuss that we handled in the store, after that she has been following me around town. This morning she was in the store. She got very upset at me when I kidded her that we had to stop meeting like this. She stormed out of the store. A little while later I went out to my car and found a very weird note under my wiper blades. I think that I have the beginning of a stalking situation."

"I tell you what. I'll come by and look at the note and talk to anyone that saw the incident this morning. We'll get something on paper. It is hard to do much about an overzealous person until they cross certain lines. I'll see you in an hour or so."

The phone rang as soon as I had put it down. "Good Samaritan's how can I help you?"

"Sam, it's Fatty, do you have a minute?"

"Sure, go ahead."

"I have some preliminary information on Patricia Jones. She is an interesting subject. There is a history of mental illness, including at least one stint in a mental health facility. The criminal background check shows lots of traffic violations and misdemeanors. A few short term stays in local jails. Stalking and domestic violence charges, later dropped. She has an erratic employment history. Her connection with The Good Samaritan Society is fairly recent. Less than a year. Sam, there is more. I'll drop off what I have tomorrow."

"That's great Fatty, keep digging. Another job, Lori Smalls. I don't have much on her except she is local. Anything that you can dig up will be appreciated. Thanks, I'll talk to you tomorrow." I feel better, now that I have him looking into Lori, too!

There was a knock on my door. I opened the door to find Sgt. Dargey standing there. "Come in, thanks for being so prompt." I handed him the note.

"Is Doug available?"

"I think so. Let me page him." We made small talk as we waited for Doug.

"I will have some information on Ms. Jones. I was able to get my friend to look her up. From the overview, there might be something useful in it."

"Call me when you have it. Wetzl and I will take a look at what you found." There was a tap at my door. I opened it, ushering Doug in.

"Nice to see you again, Doug. If it's alright, can I ask you a few questions about Lori Smalls?"

"Sure, but I've only talked to her a handful of times since we reconnected." Dargey showed Doug the note.

"That is Lori's handwriting. She used to give me little notes about everything. It was almost compulsive. If I did something she didn't like, I got a note. When we were together, she became annoyed at the weirdest little things, so I got lots of notes." He laughed.

"Since the two of you reconnected, has Lori made any odd statements about Sam?"

"No, like I told Sam, she just said that he was a nice guy. I do know that when her and I were together back in school, she showed up at everything that I was doing. After we started dating, she was by my side everywhere I went. That's why it was such a shock when I found out she was cheating on me." Doug kind of slumped down as he spoke of her cheating. It was still an open wound.

"Sam, Doug, I think that is all I need today. Doug thank you for your forthright comments." Doug quietly stood up and departed.

"I think that is still a hard spot for him."

"You may be right; Sam. Ms. Smalls seems to be a repeat offender. This, plus the ex-wife, are adding up to trouble, but I don't know which of you is going to be on the receiving end."

"That just confirms my smell meter. I knew something was out of whack. Thanks again. I'll call when I have the information that we discussed."

"Linda, roundup Angela and Amy, so we can tell them our decision."

"I'll get them right over." I only waited a few minutes before Linda reappeared at my door.

"Angela come on in." When everybody was settled, I began. "Angela, we have made our decision. At this time, we've chosen Amy, but it was a close decision. At this time, we feel Amy is better suited to move to Enumclaw. You are our choice to become the Head Cashier. The job will give you a bump in pay and responsibility. I feel that you are one of our best employees."

"That's a load off my mind. I couldn't take the job at this time. What does this new position entail?"

"After the meeting, Linda will have a packet with the details of the position. Once again thank you for your hard work." Angela departed. Amy came in.

"Good morning, Amy. Linda and I would like to inform you that you are our choice for the new Enumclaw manager's job, congratulations."

"I really didn't think that I had a chance. Angela has so much more experience. I think that I'll do a good job. What happens now?"

"Linda will give you a packet with the information about pay and benefits. When she is done with explaining the packets to you and Angela, we'll be going to Enumclaw to introduce you."

"When will I start?"

"Tomorrow, if everything works out. Again, thank you for your good work."

"Linda, after you finish bringing them up to speed, we'll head to Enumclaw. I'll be in the store."

Linda went to do her thing. I went out to walk around the store. The store was full of shoppers, but I didn't see any regulars. I started back to the furniture section. There was only one customer in the section. She turned towards me. Lori Smalls locked eyes with me. She seemed panicked. There was only one way out of the furniture area; through me.

"Sam, I'd like to apologize for my actions yesterday. I seem to be unable to control my thoughts and emotions. It has been hard since Doug came back. Then I met you and you were so kind to me. I'm so lonely, most of the time, that I have trouble seeing what is happening. I can't afford counseling, yet I need it."

"Lori, maybe I can help. See the Society office back there. The people in the office can find an affordable counselor for you."

"Oh, Sam Simone thinks that I need counseling. Who are you to judge me?" Lori ran screaming and muttering out the door, once again.

"Sam, you have a way with women." Linda had a sad look on her face.

"She needs help. It's beyond me what to do."

"I didn't mean to be flip, but she is really out of it."

"I know, I have a little experience, with out of it women."

"Well, let's head to Enumclaw." We made our way to the door.

As we pulled out of the parking lot, I noticed a woman sitting in a car in the lot of the little burger place. Her car was parked facing Good Sam's. If I'm not mistaken, it was Pat Jones. I guess that they're taking turns annoying me. I didn't mention anything because I'm not sure that it was her.

Linda and Amy enjoyed a nice conversation as we headed to Enumclaw. I didn't add anything to their conversation. As we entered the outskirts of Enumclaw,

Linda commented. "Sam, are you okay? You haven't uttered a word. That's not like you."

"Well, I wasn't going to bring it up, but as we pulled out of Good Sam's, I thought that I saw Pat Jones sitting in a car at The Little Burger Shop."

"You saw the ex-wife, are you sure?"

"Not completely, but I'm pretty sure it was her. I guess that they're going to take turns being obnoxious."

"Well, we're almost to Enumclaw, don't let it ruin your day."

"So, Amy, you've been going to school while working. That's pretty cool, what are your academic goals?"

"I want to get a bachelor degree in Business or Management."

"I got my bachelor's while working and having kids. It's tough, but doable. Just keep plugging."

"Thanks, Sam. I need all the encouragement that I can get."

"If you ever need some help finishing school, just talk to me and I'll see what we can do." I said as I pulled into a parking spot right by the front door of the store.

"Last week, we had to hike to the store. Good job, Bossman."

"Don't be a smart aleck. I usually park close. Last week was an unusual alignment of the parking gods."

"Sam, you're full of it." Everyone was in a good mood, including me, as we went in.

Amanda and Jenny were both working. They looked up to see us come in.

"Morning, everybody. I see that you brought a friend."

"Amanda, Jenny, this Amy Brown. Our choice for the new Enumclaw manager."

"It's nice to meet you. I hope that you enjoy working in Enumclaw as much as I did."

"Amy, I'm Jenny. I'm looking forward to working with you and getting to know you."

"Thank you, both of you, I've talked to both of you on the phone, so it is a pleasure to put faces to the voices." The rest of the day went very smoothly. The women got to know each other. When I told Jenny that we were giving her a raise. She hugged me. I believe that if you treat your employees with grace and appreciation that they will give it back to the job over and over again.

When it was time to head back to Auburn, I felt pretty good about the transition in Enumclaw. Linda and I had made the right choice for the job. Amy would start tomorrow in her new job. Amanda had nearly two weeks before her departure. Linda and I would discuss the need to replace Amy in the store when we returned. With a lot of smiles and hugs, we said our goodbyes before heading back to Auburn.

It was four when we drove into the parking lot. Bob was waiting at the front of the store when we walked in. He didn't look very happy.

"Can I talk to both of you?"

"Sure Bob, step into my office." Amy went back to empty her locker. We stepped into my office.

"We've had a problem all day. That Pat woman has been harassing customers from the sidewalk and the burger place across the street. At first, I tried to ignore her, but she got more brazen as the day went on. Customers were complaining about her harassment."

"Bob, did you call the police?"

"Yes, but the dispatcher told me that there wasn't much that they could do."

"Okay, I'll follow up with the police and make sure that they know that this is an ongoing case of harassment. You did exactly what you're supposed to do. Bob did you get a description of her car or her license plate?"

"Yes, it's all down on this notepad." He pointed at a notepad on my desk. I sat down and called Sgt. Dargey's cell phone.

"This is Sgt. Dargey, how can I help you?"

"This is Sam Simone. I need to report some harassment from Pat Jones. Our assistant manager, Bob, called dispatch to report the incident, but they told him that there wasn't much that they could do. I would like to make sure the incident gets reported. We have a license number and a description of her car."

"Give me what you have. I'll try to come by and talk to Bob, but it might be tomorrow." I gave him the information. Pat Jones seemed to be trying to create havoc every few days. Of the two women, Pat was much more aggressive, but Lori was more personal in her actions. I couldn't decide which one was more dangerous.

THE UNKNOWN

A car sat across the street from a small house on the north end of Auburn. The woman in the car was gathering information before making her next move. She had been planning her revenge for over five years. Her marriage had started unraveling when the woman contacted her about a child. A child that may not even be her ex-husband's. Doug never knew about the child. She had chased off the woman and her claims of paternity. It still ruined her marriage. She couldn't forget that Doug had never told her about this Lori.

After their divorce, Doug disappeared into thin air. She had spent over five years looking for him. It was by accident that she found him back in his hometown. The hardest part after finding him was getting a legitimate way to show up there.

This Sam Simone had ended her cover, but he would be a third part of her revenge. She had been very busy following each of her targets. Twice, she had been inside Lori's house. Lori's son would be better off without a mother that didn't even know who her son's dad was.

Lori got off work and headed to her parent's house. They were planning a trip to California. Little Doug was going with his grandparents. She wanted to double check what the boy would need for the trip. Her parents had started a tradition of taking Doug with them at least once a year. This year they would go down the coast seeing the sights and visiting relatives. They were scheduled to leave on Saturday. Lori didn't have enough vacation time to go with them, so she thought of it as a vacation from parenting. She felt lucky to have such good parents. They didn't blink an eye when she announced that she was pregnant. They just stepped up and helped her and their grandson.

Doug walked into his small house and flopped down on his recliner. It had been a busy day at the store. The good thing was that the store sold four appliances. Doug needed a little something to brighten his mood. His two biggest failures had showed up at the same time. This had spooked him. He knew that he was bound to run into Lori, but Pat, also showing up, was scary. As he sat trying to relax, he felt like someone was there. He got up and looked around. Things seemed to be a little out of place.

Pat returned to her hotel to start putting her plans into place. Her life had always been in an uproar. Whenever things went wrong the noise in her head played at full volume. The pain wouldn't subside until she found a way to fix the problem. The disintegration of her marriage had been roaring in her head for over five years. At times, she didn't function at all. Just getting on the plane to fly to Seattle had used up most of her ability to appear normal. She wasn't prepared to go into the Good Samaritan's store and come face to face with Doug. All she knew was that he had returned to his hometown. Her reaction had caused her to lose her job. It pushed her to change her original plans. She was winging it and trying to hold onto her last shred of sanity.

I sat down to look over all the information Fatty had dug up for me. There was a mountain of information on Pat Jones, not so much on Lori Smalls. Fatty was very thorough. After an hour of reading the files, I came to one conclusion; Pat was an extremely troubled individual. The info on Lori didn't give me much of a picture of her, but Pat had a long history of mental health breakdowns. It surprised me that she had been able to land any job, let alone the one with the Good Samaritan Society.

The Big A wasn't very crowded on a Wednesday evening. Timmy was sitting at the bar waiting for Jody. An attractive woman sat down next to him. Timmy noticed that she seemed extremely nervous.

"How are you this fine night?" She asked Tim.

"I'm doing alright."

"I've heard a lot about this place, my ex-husband used to talk about it a lot. I just got in town, so I thought I'd check it out." She had become more at ease as she talked to Tim.

"Who's your ex? Maybe I know him."

"Doug Toms. We've been divorced for years."

"What brings you to Auburn?"

"I came to look over Good Samaritan Stores."

"I love Good Sam's. I've been going there for years. Great place. They do a lot for the needy." Tim's intuition was picking up some bad vibes. This woman was looking for something about Good Sam's.

"We're evaluating the management at all of our stores. Do you know Sam, the manager?"

"Can't say that I do. I might know him by sight, but I've never met the manager." Her demeanor changed abruptly.

"I heard that he's very outgoing. That everyone knows him. I really need to get some background on him. It would really help me out."

"Sorry, like I said, I don't know him. I wish that I could help."

"I think that you're a liar. You could help me, but you're a lying asshole."

"I don't know what your problem is, but you have over stayed your welcome. John, eighty-six our friend."

"Okay, out you go." John took a picture to put her face on the hall of shame.

"You can't treat me like this. I'll have your job."

Jody came out while John was escorting the now screaming woman out the door. "What's going on?"

"I'm not sure, except that I think Sam has someone trying to stir up trouble." Tim and Jody went into the office. Tim made a call on his phone.

"Hey Tim, what's up?"

"Sam, can you come to the Big A? I need to show you a picture. It will only take a few minutes."

"Sure, I'll be right there."

"Where are you going?"

"Tim has something that he wants to show me. I'll only be gone a few minutes." I kissed Jude as I went out the door.

The Big A was half empty when I pulled up. I spotted Tim as I walked in. He waved me over.

"Buy you a drink?"

"That sounds good, make it a diet cola." The drink appeared on the bar. "What's on your mind, Tim?"

"Well, a woman came in asking a lot of questions about Good Sam's and if I knew the manager. She wouldn't take no for an answer when I told her that I didn't know you. This woman got upset and called me a lying asshole. I took offense to her accusations and kicked her out. I had John take her picture, you know for our Wall of Shame."

"You have a Wall of Shame?"

"I think we do, but I wanted a picture so you can see who's going after you." Tim showed me the picture.

"That's Patricia Jones. She used to work for the Good Samaritan's national office. She also used to be married to Doug Tom, our appliance repairman. I think that she is dangerous and crazy. I just don't know what she is up to."

"You live such an abnormal life."

"Not by choice, not by choice."

"If you need any help, just say the word, okay!"

"How's little Samantha? I haven't been over to see her for a while."

"She's growing like a weed. This parenthood thing is a hoot. It may be the coolest thing that I've ever done."

"Tell Jody that I said hi. Give the little one a kiss from Uncle Sam. I'll get back to you about Ms. Jones. Thank you again Tim."

I headed out the door. I made sure that I took a good look around the parking lot. I didn't see anything out of the ordinary. All I knew was that I wished that I had a clue about what Pat was up to.

CRAZY CAR DAYS

My visit with Tim left me very troubled. I slept in fits. My alarm woke me up, but it didn't take much effort to get me up, as I was right at the edge of waking all night. My shower knocked some of the sleepiness out of me. Slowly, I wandered to the kitchen.

"Sam, are you feeling okay?" Jude looked at me with worried eyes.

"I don't know. These two women are dragging my mind through the dirt. Physically, I'm feeling fine, but my mind is being overrun with bad thoughts."

"Why don't you take a day off and clear your head?"

"I wish that I could, but there's too much going on for me to stay home. I think that the car will be ready today, too!"

"Try to have a good day. Call me if you need anything."

"Where's Joey? He's supposed to take me to work in case that the car is ready."

"He's getting something from his room." Joey walked into the kitchen as we were speaking.

"Ready Dad?"

"Yeah, let's go." We all departed at the same time. Neither, Joey or I had much to say on the way to work.

"Thanks, Joey. I'll let you know if the shop calls."

"Sure, Dad. You know where to find me. Have a good day." The way that I felt, that would be easier said than done.

I got a phone call from the repair shop telling me that Marie's car was finished. I made arrangements to pick it up after work. It felt like the day was improving, so I decided to go to the warehouse and talk to Joey about the car and talk to Bob about bikes. I figured to kill two birds with one stone, sort of.

I spotted Bob as I walked into the warehouse. I decided to start with him. Bob was supervising some employees as they loaded a truck for deliveries.

"Hey, Bob do you have a minute?"

"Sure, Sam. We can talk at the break table." I followed him into the breakroom.

"Linda told me that you'd like a chance to be the new bike guy."

"Yes, I figured that if we set it up the way it was before, that I had a chance of making a little money out of the job."

"Were you planning on repairing them here?"

"That was my general idea. I would work on them in the morning and a half-day on one of my days off."

"That works for me. Let me know what you'll need to get started."

"I'll bring you my list of things by, Friday."

"That will be fine. Kids need bikes." I got up and headed to the appliance room. I stood in the doorway for a moment watching Joey work on a washer. He seemed to be putting it back together. The odd thing was Doug was nowhere to be seen.

"What are you working on?" Joey looked up surprised to see me.

"I started this washer yesterday; I'm putting it back together. The pump was bad. It should work like new."

"Where's Doug?"

"I don't know. He hasn't been in all morning."

"Well, that's good to know. The car is finished. I'll need a ride over towards closing time."

"That's great. Can I just work until closing time? Ginger is visiting her grandmother."

"Sure, work on what you need to for your classes and the store." I headed back to the store. I needed to talk to Linda. She was pulling items to put in the discount area.

"What do you need, Sam?"

"Did you get a call from Doug this morning?"

"No, isn't he here?"

"No. I just went over to tell Joey that I needed a ride to get Marie's car. No Doug."

"Do you want me to call him?"

"Yes, he's supposed to call you when he lays-off."

"I'll call him and let you know, okay?"

"Suzie, I think my Dad bought me a car."

"How do you know that?"

"Well, I caught my Dad talking on the phone about picking up something at the garage. When I walked into the room, he got off the phone real fast."

"I hope that's what it is, but you could be in for a big disappointment, too! Do you have an idea what type of car it might be?"

"No. I can't wait to finish driver's training. If I don't have a car, I'll never get to drive." Suzie was giving Marie a ride home from soccer practice.

"I can't tell if Mr. Jones likes me. He keeps moving me around to different positions."

"I don't care if he likes me. He is a big improvement over Cummings. Remember what my Dad always says, if your versatile, you'll find a way onto the field."

"That's easy for you to say, you can score and play defense better than just about anyone out there."

"Most of the varsity will be girls off the Roadrunners. Most of us were varsity last season. The best season Twin Rivers has ever had. Just relax. You'll be fine."

"I hope so. Thanks, you always prop me up when I'm down."

"What are friends for?"

Joey finished the washer he was working on. He began a couple of warranty jobs that needed to go back to the customers. The day was busy, but fulfilling. Doug had enough manuals to help him through a few tight spots. The warranty jobs were finished by lunch. Joey went to find Bob.

"Bob, who do I let know when warranty repairs are finished?"

"Linda takes care of making the arrangements." He headed into the store to find Linda. Linda was helping at the counter when he spotted her.

"Linda, do you have a minute?"

"Sure, Joey. What do you need?"

"I finished two warranty repairs."

"Come into my office. I'll look up the details." They went to her office. "Have a seat. Do you have the work orders?"

"Right here." Linda looked up each order. Everything looked okay.

"Thanks Joey, I'll set up the return delivery. Put these tags on the items. You seem to be catching on really fast. It's too bad Doug seems to be having some issues. That reminds me, I have to call him. Anything else?"

"No, I just wanted to finish the warranties." Joey went back to the shop. Linda called Doug. Doug's phone went right to leave a message.

"Rockstar, what are you looking up?"

"I'm looking up that woman that's been harassing Sam. Something smells about her."

"You do know that there are two women stalking or harassing Sam. Both are connected to his appliance guy, Doug."

"How do you know that?"

"I have my ways. I ran into Jude at the market." Jody laughed as she went back to work.

I looked at the clock. Nearly four-thirty. I finished what I was doing and went to get Joey. I stopped and told Linda that I was leaving, before I left. Joey was busy working on a dishwasher as I entered the shop. Looking around, I saw that he had finished at least three more repairs. He finally noticed that I was standing in the doorway. "Hey Dad, I'll be finished in a minute."

"Go ahead and finish your project, we have plenty of time to get the car." It took Joey just a couple of minutes to finish and put away the tools.

"I'm ready. I had a good day. I finished all the warranty work, before starting the dishwasher. I'll have it ready for the store tomorrow."

"I'm impressed. Good job. Let's go get your sister her new car." I gave Joey a playful slap on the back as we left the shop. As we hopped into Joey's car, I remembered the look on his face when I showed him this car nearly three years ago. It was priceless.

Joey pulled into the Auto Service Center. I spotted Marie's car right away. It was parked right in front of the store. "Is that it, Dad?"

"I think so. That looks nothing like the car, even before the damage."

"If Marie doesn't like that car, I'll take it and give her mine." We both laughed. I went to the counter to pay the bill. Joey went to look at the car.

"Sam, it looks pretty good. Everything is done."

"Bill, you guys did a great job on the paint. That doesn't look like the same car. I think my son might be a little jealous. He's looking it over like a lovesick calf."

"Thanks for the compliments. The invoice is ready. It came in about fifty dollars lower, so that's an added surprise." Bill showed me the bill as I paid for the work. I went outside to tell Joey we were ready to go home.

"Follow me home, just in case. Maybe your sister will let you drive it after she gets a first chance at driving it."

"I'll have to bribe her with my charm."

The Elantra started right up. I backed out and we started for home. The car drove really nice, plus it had power everything. By the time we pulled into the driveway, I think that I'd made a very good choice for Marie. David was watching out the window. He started the daddy dance as soon as he figured out that it was me. Within seconds, David was pulling Marie and Jude out the door.

"Oh my God! Is it really mine?" The look on Marie's face said it all. Jude was smiling as she recorded the happy scene.

"Yes, it's yours." She almost knocked me down to give me a hug. The Simone's were having a happy celebration for Marie's first car. Jude came over and gave me a quick kiss. I guess that I passed all the tests.

"Can I drive it?"

"That's the idea. Have you started dinner?"

"Not yet, why?"

"I'll treat at *Rome's Best Pizza.* I think that we can all fit in the car. What do you say?"

"That sounds like a plan. Get David's seat and I'll lock the door. The Simone's were soon off to eat pizza in celebration of Marie's new car.

DOWN TO BUSINESS

It was sunny as the Simones began the preparations for a new day. Marie was still glowing with happiness from getting a car from her parents. Joey's confidence grew every day with school and appliance training. David had made a friend in his first day at school. Jude was happy to see the kids so happily thriving. I guess that I was the only one that wasn't living on the upside. The troubles with Doug's girls or ex-girls was starting to wear on me. I didn't want to rain on everybody's parade, so I'm trying to get my crap together.

"Eggs or waffles, your choice Sam?"

"Eggs would be my choice. How are the Simones this morning?" That brought on an explosion of comments from my brood. That made me feel better. The eggs and toast were soon served. I devoured them. Maybe, I could have a good day.

I was in luck. The radio blasted some Burton Cummings as my trusty T-Bird carried me to work. The euphoria was soon burst. The front door of Good Sam's was cracked and graffitied. The crew that beat me to work were waiting outside. I called 911 and got out.

"Who was here first?"

"I was Sam. I kept everyone away from the door."

"Thanks, Bob. When did you get here?"

"About ten minutes ago."

"Bob, take the crew around to the warehouse rear entrance. I'll wait for the police. Linda and I will send the rest of the crew around."

"Linda, is Fatty supposed to work today?"

"I'm pretty sure that he is. Have him check the camera to see if we can get a shot of our intruder."

"Camera, what camera?"

"The one that Fatty installed after the trouble with George and my ex happened."

"Who knew about this camera?"

"Well, you, me and Fatty. We're trying to keep it as secret as we possible."

"With you, there's always something." Linda went away shaking her head. She returned as Auburn's finest arrived. An officer emerged from his car. I didn't recognize him.

"Who made the complaint?"

"I did. I'm Sam Simone, the manager, let me show you the damage." The young patrolman looked at the door. He took a few photos as he checked things out.

"Did they get into the store?"

"Not that we can tell, the door was still locked with the alarm set. I believe that this is connected to some harassment that the store has gotten from a woman named Patricia Jones."

"Do you have any proof that this Jones person did this?"

"No, we're waiting to see what was captured on the camera. The camera results should be ready anytime. Sgt. Dargey and Officer Wetzl have been handling the other harassment and damages calls."

"Okay, I have pictures of the damage, if the camera shows what happened, call and ask for me. My name is John McBee, here's my card."

"Thank you, we'll be in touch." The officer departed as we tried to go back to normal, or as normal as we could be with a start like this.

"Bob, call the contractors. Linda, let's try to open on time, if possible. I need to speak with Fatty." I went to find Fatty. He was hard at work in the testing room.

"Sam, I'm just bringing up the footage, grab a chair." I sat down and waited for the show. The camera system hadn't been needed since Fatty put it together. That's a good thing, because if we had needed to check, it would just mean something bad had happened.

"Here goes." The screen showed what a quiet night looked like, until around five. A car pulled into the lot and stopped right in front of the door. The weird thing was that the car was definitely Lori Smalls car, but the woman that stepped out wasn't Lori, it was Pat Jones. Pat went right about her business. She hit the door with a little sledge hammer. When she cracked the glass, she took some paint cans out of the car and graffitied the window. She picked up her tools and climbed back into Lori's car. The whole scene took about five minutes.

"That worked as advertised. Can you zoom in on the car and get a shot of the license plate. After that, get a clear shot of her face."

"Child's play. I'll have them in about ten minutes."

"I'll be back. Now, I just have to figure out why Pat was driving Lori's car. I can't see those two working together. I have a bad feeling about Lori."

Pat was very pleased with her plans, so far. The police should be looking at Lori for the problems at Good Sam's. Her car is clearly in view of any camera. It may take a few days before anyone discovers that Doug is missing. No one knows about the little place that she rented in Doug's name. The two occupants are secured in the large basement. There are no neighbors within a mile of the place. Once Pat finishes with Sam, she'll take care of Lori and Doug. Hopefully, no one checks out the little place in the country until she is far, far away.

Two Auburn police cars pulled into The Good Samaritan parking lot. Sgt. Dargey and Officer McBee emerged from their cars and walked in.

"Is Sam in?" Dargey asked Angela.

"Yes, I'll call him." I responded to the page and went to the counter.

"Gentlemen, I have some video to show you. Please, follow me." We walked to area where Fatty was set up and waiting for us. We gathered around the screen. Fatty started the show. Everyone was silent as we watched the screen.

"Okay, Sam, I can see that Patricia Jones is the perpetrator, but what else are we supposed to see?"

"Fatty, bring up the car." The car appeared with a closeup of the license plate. "That's not Pat's car. That is Lori Small's car."

"Run that number. Do you have an idea what that means?"

"I believe that Pat is trying to point a finger at Lori. I don't think that they would work together. I think Lori is kind of a little off. Pat seems to be a bonafide loon."

"Let's see if you're right about the car before we make any guesses about this." It soon came back that the car was registered to Lori Smalls.

"Bob, can you run by the Smalls woman's house?"

"Yeah, I'll get right on it."

"I'd like to talk to Doug again."

"Sure, his shop is right back there." McBee left to visit Lori and we headed to the appliance shop. As we entered the shop, I noticed that Joey was the only one in there.

"Hey, dad, what do you need?" Joey was smiling as he looked up.

"We need to talk to Doug."

"He's not here. I haven't seen him since Friday."

"Thanks, Joey." We went back to my office.

"Do you have Doug's address?"

"Sure, here it is. Can you let me know if you find him?"

"I'll give you a call." Sgt. Dargey left. I went to find Linda.

"Linda, Doug is missing again today. Did you ever talk to him?"

"No, I've been calling every couple of hours with no success. I should have told you. My bad."

"It's just puzzling that he's missing. Pat was our person this morning. The cameras caught her, but the odd thing is that she was driving Lori Smalls car."

"Does that mean the two are in cahoots?"

"I don't think so, but the police are checking some things right now."

WHERE HAS EVERYONE GONE

Bob McBee stopped in front of the small rambler. The yard needed mowing and the house looked like it had seen better days. He approached the door with caution. The case was weird enough to make him use extra care as he knocked on the door. His impulses told him that Lori Smalls was in as much danger as Doug Toms. He couldn't explain why he thought that they were in danger from the ex-wife, just that they were. No one answered his knock. He looked in the windows, before walking around to the back yard. He saw Lori's car from the side garage window. As he came back around to the front a neighbor came to the front gate.

"If you're looking for Lori, I think she moved. I saw a woman helping her take some things and go a few days ago."

"If I showed you a picture, could you tell me if it was the woman that you saw?"

"I suppose so. Lori has been my neighbor and friend for a long time. Has something happened to her?"

"I don't know, but people that move don't usually leave their car behind. Tell me if this is the woman that you saw." The woman looked at the photo. She made no comment at first, but Officer McBee saw her facial expression when she looked at the picture.

"That's the woman I saw. I had never seen her before. She seemed to be in control of Lori. I wish that I'd spoken up, but I was kind of mad that she would go away without so much as a goodbye."

"It may turn out to be nothing, but it gives us a start to find out what has happened. Don't be so hard on yourself. Can I get your name and address for my report?" Bonny Johnson was very helpful as she gave her information.

Sgt. Dargey pulled up the long driveway to Doug Tom's house. The house sat in the middle of a couple acres filled with appliances. There was an outbuilding on the side of the house. Dargey felt it was the shop. Most of the appliances surrounded this building. He carefully got out of the car, checking for dogs. He heard them barking, but couldn't see a kennel. He gingerly made his way to the house. The place looked abandoned. The doorbell set off a second wave of barking. The only thing moving inside was one of those yappy little dogs. Next, he went to check the shop. He didn't think anyone was there. The noise was enough to wake the dead. The shop was padlocked tight. He found the kennel on the side of the shop. It contained one very sad looking dog. There wasn't any food or water left in the bowls. He contacted animal control to help take care of the animals.

The house had been quiet for a long time. Lori was awake but groggy. She was bound and gagged. Her mask had slipped enough for her to see another person in the room. It was a man. The man was still out. Lori couldn't remember what happened. She had dropped off her son for his trip and returned home. As she walked in the front door, something exploded in her head. Everything was blurry after that. She studied the man snoring loudly on the floor next to her. It was Doug. What was going on? She didn't have any enemies. Who would want to hurt her and Doug?

There was noise coming from outside the room. The door opened. A woman that looked like Doug's ex-wife came through the door.

"I see that one of you has woke from your sleep. I suppose that you want to know what's happening? You two have caused me a lot of pain. I need to end the pain. It's simple, when you both cease to exist, my pain will go away." Pat backed out the door. Lori noticed that the room had no windows, just the one door. She couldn't imagine what was on the other side of the door.

GONE BUT NOT FORGOTTEN

I sat down at my desk. The phone was blinking. It looked like that I had two messages. I grabbed a pen and pushed the playback button.

"Sam, this is Sgt. Dargey. After checking at Doug Tom's house. It looks like he's been gone for a while. His dogs had no food or water. His car is gone. I've made arrangements for taking care of his dogs. A missing person's report has been filed. That's all that I can tell you right now." The message ended. The next one started to play.

"Mr. Simone, this is Officer McBee. I have some disturbing news about Ms. Smalls. As I was checking out the property, a woman came out and told me that she thought Ms. Smalls had moved. As we talked, the neighbor mentioned that a woman was helping her. I showed the woman a picture of Pat Jones. The neighbor identified Pat Jones as the woman helping Smalls. The neighbor was upset that Lori didn't even say goodbye. I will be talking to my supervisors about the situation." The messages turned off.

I pulled out a folder from my filing cabinet. I quickly found the file that I needed. I had a bad feeling about Doug and Lori. There wasn't much that I could do about them at the moment, but I needed to replace Doug; temporarily. There were a couple of previous appliance graduates that might be able to step in. Getting us through the problem until we knew more about Doug's plight. Joe Johnson answered on the first ring. I explained what I needed. He agreed to help us out. Joe was the second apprentice to finish the program. Now he owned a very successful appliance shop. Joe would be in tomorrow to see what we needed.

I went out to look for Linda. The store was very busy, so I jumped in helping where I was needed. It gave me a little reprieve from all the bad thoughts about Doug and Lori. As I was helping, I noticed a couple of bikes sitting by the appliance area. During a small break in the action, I went and looked them over. They looked like new. Bob came in with some new stuff for the store. He delivered the items before stopping at the bikes.

"How do you like them, Sam?"

"These are yours?"

"Yeah, I decided to just get started with what I already had. They came out pretty good, huh?"

"I should say so. They're better than good. I'm impressed."

"Thanks, Sam. I'll have some more done in a few days."

I went back to my office. Linda was at my door as I walked up. "I started out looking for you, but it looked like that the crew was swamped with customers. Now I remember what I wanted to talk to you about. Do you have a minute?"

"Sam, I always have a minute for you. What's up?"

"Quite a few things. I guess that I'll start with the messages from Sgt. Dargey and Officer McBee. Dargey said that Doug's place looked abandoned. His dogs had no water or food. His car is missing. When McBee got to Lori's house, a neighbor came out and said that she thought that Lori had moved. McBee showed her a picture of Pat. The woman identified Pat as the woman helping Lori move. Lori's car was in the garage out back. The neighbor was upset that Lori didn't even say goodbye. They had been back fence friends for years.

I have contacted Joe Johnson to see if he could help us with the appliance program temporarily. He'll be in tomorrow to see what we need. Bob has started the bike program, already. I think that his first bikes are very good." I felt wound down as I finished my thoughts.

"I don't know where to start. The Doug and Lori situation sounds very serious. I don't feel good about it ending well.

If I remember right, Joe may have been the best graduate of the appliance program. I hope he decides to help out even if it's just temporarily.

I saw the bikes. I agree that Bob did a wonderful job on them. My fingers are crossed. I hope it is a good addition to the store."

"I would like you and Bob to sit in on the meeting with Joe. Joe is very busy with his store, so if we can give him as much support as possible it will go a long way to not losing too many sales in appliances."

"You know that son of yours seems to have a knack for fixing appliances. It may help him to show what he's capable of."

"Those thoughts have crossed my mind, too!" Linda went back to work. I sat just thinking for a few minutes. Something was nagging me, but it was just out of my reach. I was scared for Doug and Lori, but I felt that Pat wasn't finished creating havoc.

Doug was still semi-unconscious; Lori had lost track of time. She wasn't sure how long that they had been there. If

Doug didn't start coming around soon, she feared that he may not survive. Inside, she believed that their captor was Pat, but she wasn't sure. The woman had never shown her face. But Pat was the only one with a connection to both her and Doug. At the time she had contacted Doug, about her child, he and Pat were still married. Doug claimed that he never heard anything about the child, but that his marriage had crumbled in that time-frame.

Pat was sitting down the street from Good Sam's. She was driving a different car with borrowed plates. Lori's car was sitting in the garage. Pat needed to blend in while she plotted her revenge on Sam. She spent her days watching Sam's every move. He would be harder to track and punish. Sam was a more experienced and intelligent target. She was surprised how fast he had ruined her plan to remove him from the store.

Tim was watching his daughter playing in her playpen. Fatherhood had struck a chord with him. Jody ran the bar and when he didn't have any commitments, he took care of their child. It was the best of worlds for him. Today, Tim was waiting for conformation about the woman that had come looking for Sam. Tim had put his team into motion to find her and keep Sam safe. The ringing of the doorbell brought Tim out of his deep thoughts.

"Come on in Jason. Make yourself at home. Would you like some coffee or soda?"

"Some cola would hit the spot."

"Coming right up." Tim returned with a couple of sodas and a bottle for Samantha.

"She's growing like a weed. You've got a cute kid, Tim."

"I like her, I'll think I'll keep her."

"We have a good idea where Pat Jones is hiding. If she's got the other two people, it is perfect for holding them. I have people watching the place, plus we've been following her as she follows Simone. If she makes a move on him, we are prepared to intervene."

"I need to talk with Sam. Keep up what you're doing. I will contact you after I speak with Sam. Good work as always, Jason." They chatted for a while like the old friends that they were.

I made it to work a little early. Being antsy from not sleeping well. It seemed that I just couldn't get my mind off of what had happened over the last few weeks. I knew it had to be connected to Pat Jones, but I was unable to fill in the gaps. Somewhere, if they're still alive, Pat has them hidden. Trying to find them was like looking for a needle in a haystack. The main thing gnawing at me was that Pat seemed to be coming after me. That's the thoughts that I couldn't shake. I hope to be amped down a little by the time Joe arrived for our meeting.

Joe walked in just as we opened. He never seems to change. When he came in to apply for the program, he had just graduated and was trying to figure out what he wanted to do with his life. He had personality-plus. Everyone took an instant liking to him. Ross liked him so much, that he gave him extra time. Joe was ready to graduate long before his training was over. I remember a few months after that, Joe showed up to tell me that he had leased a place to open up his first store. Today, I heard that he has three stores.

"Morning Joe, thanks for coming in. I think that we'll have our meeting in the appliance shop. Linda and Bob will be joining us." We headed to the shop. Soon, we were all settled.

"I guess the place to start is with the reason that we need your help. Doug, our current appliance man has disappeared. We are pretty much in the dark as to what happened to him. The store needs someone to fill in. The apprentice program is in full swing. The store is always in need of products from this shop. We don't need someone to be here full-time, but maybe six hours in the afternoon. Our student needs a journeyman repairman to sign off on his hours for the college."

"I have an idea, Sam. I could rotate a couple of my qualified repairmen and myself, to help get you through this tight spot. I can send their credentials to the college. I think that my company would be happy to give back to the place that gave me my start."

"That would be a godsend, Joe. How soon can you get this started?"

"I'd like to meet the apprentice. If I can get an idea where he's at training wise, I can see what I'll need to look at for trainers."

"He'll be in at one. His name is Joey. That's Joey Simone."

"Your boy, Sam?"

"Yes." We worked out a few more details before Joe left, promising to be back at one.

I was working on some changes that I had in mind for the store, when I looked up and saw Tim smirking at me.

"You get pretty engrossed in your work, Hoss. It wouldn't take much to have disabled you and you'd be sitting with your missing friends." When Tim called me Hoss, I knew he was being serious.

"What brings the Rock God all the way to this part of town?"

"If you have a minute, I'll tell you."

"Come in. Shut the door. Let me have what you've found."

"My people have been watching the crazy woman. She has been following you every day for a week. I would assume that you're her next target. We have a good lead on where she is hiding. The only problem is that we don't know if Doug and Lori are there. I have enough people on the job to keep you secure. The hard part will be to get in and find the hostages or bodies."

"Gawd, if you weren't already my oldest, best friend, you'd be him now. I knew that I was being followed, but the car was different each time that I spotted her. You say that you have a line on where she's hiding?"

"She stopped using Lori's car after the police went to Lori's house. Pat has leased some property, but it is very secluded. My security guys are working on a plan to get closer to check for the hostages. It seems to me that whatever happens to them will go down after she deals with you. You've already messed up her original plans to get back at Doug and Lori, so we figure that she is formulating a new plan to deal with you."

"That's a lot of stuff to chew over. It's a big if, that she hasn't already dealt with them, but maybe in her agitated state, she has hopefully, put them aside to focus on me. I can't let them die. We have to come up with a way of baiting her into making a mistake." I looked at Tim. He had a faraway look. I knew that meant he was working on something to end this dilemma.

I was watching for Joey to come in. I wanted to head him off, so that he could meet Joe. Ginger's car pulled up in front of the store. Joey soon climbed out before heading in.

"Joey."

"What's up, Dad?"

"I wanted to catch you before you started. I'm bringing in a new appliance teacher, until we know what's going on with Doug. He'll be here at one."

We went into my office to wait. Joe arrived with two of his repairmen in tow. Introductions were made as we moved over to the appliance shop.

"Joe, if you need me for anything, just have Joey page me. I will be in my office catching up on some work."

About an hour later, Joe knocked on my door. "I think that we had a very productive meeting. Your son is a fast learner. He is way ahead of the course at this time. My guys have agreed to be here from one till five. Monday thru Friday. Unless, your guy comes back or you hire a replacement. My employees will on my payroll, but they will keep track of hours and test results for your apprentice."

"That's great, Joe. I appreciate you helping us out."

"That's what friends are for, maybe someday you can help me out."

"Anytime, Joe."

BAITING THE HOOK

After dinner, I was doing the dishes. I heard a car pull into the driveway. "Sam, can you get the door?"

"Right on it honey." As I made my way to the door. Looking through the peep-hole, I saw Tim and Jody.

"Come in, come in. Jude, we have company."

"I know, send Jody and Samantha to the family room. You and Tim can talk in your den."

I'm always the last to know. That might be a good thing. As Tim and I were going into my den, I could hear Jude making a fuss over Jody and the baby.

"What's going on?"

"Can't a friend visit a friend?"

"Come on, Something, must have changed since we talked."

"My guys have confirmed that there is something in the house. We don't know if it's them, but they want to go in and find out. That is where you come in. We need to distract Pat, so that we can get in and out without her getting in the way."

"What do you want me to do?"

"You and I are going to lead our pyscho on a wild goose chase. We need you to go out for an errand. It seems that Pat parks far enough down the road from Good Sam's that she wouldn't see if I hitched a ride with you."

"You have enough men to cover both?"

"We will have an adequate number to keep everyone safe. They get their paychecks from me, so you and I should be okay."

"When is all of this supposed to happen?"

"Tomorrow, if all things line up."

"Okay, I want to end all of this hogwash. But, I'm still very worried about Doug and Lori."

Tonight, was Marie's first game of the high school season. They were playing under the lights. I got home, changed my clothes, we grabbed a quick dinner before heading to the game. As a dad and coach, I always had to remind myself to be calm and cool. I can't say that I've always been completely calm and cool, but I try.

"Have you met the new coach?"

"No, I didn't have a chance to go to any of her practices, especially with all the nutty stuff going on at work."

"I hope that she plays well and doesn't get hurt."

"Me too! This will be her last year of playing school or youth soccer. My hope is that she and the team does well. I also want to go to all of her games."

"As Fred says, "If the mountain don't blow." You'll be alright." We both laughed.

"Hey, what are guys laughing at?" David always wanted to know what he had missed.

"Nothing, sweetie, Mom and Dad are just being silly." My mood improved instantly. It's great to have a family that you love. We found a parking spot not too far away from the stadium. That's a good sign. As we were walking to the entrance, we passed most of the other parents. I stopped and chatted with most of them. This season would be the end of a long journey from the five and six-year-olds that they had been. I had coached almost every girl on the varsity. We had spent a lot of time together through wins, losses, and memories. I hope that the memories are mostly fond ones.

We finally made it into the stadium. I liked to sit towards the middle of the field. Jude and I usually tried to sit away from the enthusiastic fans. That way, I didn't get mad about dumb comments and David could be as noisy as a little boy could. Jack Petty came by to say hello.

"Sam, I haven't seen any headlines lately. You must be staying out of trouble." Jack snickered as he said that.

"I've been trying to steer clear of trouble, but sometimes it comes looking for me." That was all I would be saying on my current predicament.

"Sam, I'm going to concession stand. Do you want anything?"

"Some pop, please. Are you taking the little guy?"

"What do you think? He would be pretty mad if he didn't get to pick out his treat. I'll be back in a few minutes." I just sat watching warmups. Marie spotted me and waved. They were playing last year's league champs. In previous years, they had never beat them. This game will show a lot towards what type of year they were going to have.

Jude and David came back with treats and company. Joey and Ginger stopped to say hello.

"I'm glad that you two made it. I know it's tough to come back the year after you graduated. I suppose that you'll be sitting with your friends?"

"Yes, Dad, we'll be sitting with our friends, but we needed to make sure that you found the stadium."

"Funny, Joey, go hang with your friends. Just remember, I know where you sleep." They left as the public-address announcer chimed in with the line-ups and the Pledge of Allegiance. I said a little prayer as the teams lined up for the start.

The game was very exciting. Marie scored a goal in the second or third minute. Marie and her teammates were playing with an intensity I had seldom seen in them. At the end of a 3-0 victory, Marie had a hand in all the goals. She had two goals and an assist.

"Are you Marie's parents?" A young student asked us.

"Yes, we are."

"The team wants to invite you to meet the new coach." We followed the student down to track. Most of the parents had joined us there.

"Sam, do you know what's going on?" Fred Barr asked me.

"First that I heard of it was when student came to get us."

"Parents and families, thank you for coming to the game. I'd like to introduce myself, I'm Mickey Jones. I came to the job late in the summer. So, I haven't really had any time to reach out to all of you. I come from Elma High School, where I taught and coached for five years. I wanted a chance to move closer to my roots. I grew up in Enumclaw. I want to meet all of the parents. The team has set up the order that this will go. Girls get your parents. When your name is called come forward. I'll try not to take up too much more of your time."

The names of each girl were called. Marie turned out to be the last name called.

"I'm Mickey Jones, it is a pleasure to finally meet, Marie's parents."

Marie did the honors of introducing us. "Coach, this my mom Jude, my little brother David, my older brother Joey, and my dad Sam." He seemed like a very likable man. When he got to me, he stopped and took a good look at me.

"I feel like I already know you. Your presence hangs over every practice. I knew which players that had been coached by you. Those kids need the least instruction. You saw that tonight. Marie earned our first player of the game. With a win over Eatonville the team jumped an enormous hurdle. Like I said, it's a pleasure to meet you and your family."

"Thank you, coach. It is nice to meet you, too!" The introduction ceremony ended on that note. The family headed towards the parking lot. Marie was walking on air. I think that the game and her coach's words were the answers that she needed. Joey and Ginger said goodbye and left in his car. We piled into Jude's car and headed home.

As we unloaded in front of the house, Marie gave me a hug.

"Good game, kid. One down, a bunch more to go."

"Thanks, dad." I went to bed feeling good about

Marie's soccer, but very alarmed about Pat Jones.

FISHING IN TROUBLED WATER

I was a proud papa as I headed to work. The night before still glowed around me. When my kids do well, I was always filled with happiness. These thoughts had kept the bad thoughts back. Walking to the door, the bad thoughts seemed to rise up washing away the good ones.

I worked on getting the store ready to open. No one, seemed to notice, how I was twisting and turning inside. Everyone had their own thoughts and duties to deal with. The store was ready to start the day, that's when I saw Tim helping with the morning set up.

"Hey, how long have you been here?"

"For years, you hired me back in '88."

"Funny, very funny. I seem to hire a lot of out of work comedians." We made our way to my office as the store opened.

"As soon as I get the word from my guys, we'll head out. If that's okay with you, Sam?"

"That works for me. Do you want a soda?" My best friend and I sipped our sodas and waited. We were occasionally interrupted by customers and phone calls. I started feeling a little less nervous as the morning went on. Tim's phone broke the calmness of the morning.

"Okay, we'll be out in a couple minutes." Tim looked at me and nodded. It surprised me that my nervousness left me with Tim's nod. I told Linda, that I had to run some errands. Tim and I made our way to my old T-Bird. She fired right up. My T-bird has always felt like a female. I don't have any other reason for calling it she.

"Sam, turn left out of the lot. Head south on Auburn Way. Just keep going south on Auburn Way. If we need to do anything different, my guys will let me know." I kept going south. We were soon heading to Enumclaw.

"I know that you do, so put some Kinks or Who in the stereo." Sleepwalker was on top, so it was first up.

"Is she behind us?"

"Oh, yeah. She is not very good at tailing. She was easy to spot. I just got a message that we've entered the building."

"I hope that they find Doug and Lori."

Lori was very worried. Doug hadn't moved for a long time. He was breathing, but motionless. She had kept him warm. She was doing the best that she could, but it still seemed like he was slipping away.

"Doug, wake up, please wake up! You need to eat. Please keep fighting. I'm sorry for everything that I did to you. We need to survive; we have a son that needs us." Lori began sobbing. She was on the verge of losing it herself. During her near breakdown, she heard noises in the house. Instantly, she shielded Doug. Noises and voices told her that whatever was out there, was close to the door. The door seemed to explode open. Men flooded into the room. The men soon found Doug and Lori.

The men checked them over, before carrying them to a van outside. A paramedic started working on Doug. Nothing was said to Lori. The men drove for miles. Lori had no idea where they were going. After, what seemed like hours the van came to a stop. A gurney was waiting for Doug, a wheelchair for Lori. Lori looked around. The place looked like an underground garage. She and Doug were wheeled into a medical facility. Medical personnel moved quickly to start treating Doug. A woman stepped towards Lori.

"Hello, Ms. Smalls, I'm Dr. Brady. I would like to check you out to see if everything is working after your ordeal."

"Where am I? Is Doug going to be okay? He was very sick the whole time that we were being held."

"Well, you're in a private clinic. We want to keep you safe until your abductor is taken care of. As to Mr. Toms, his medical team will report to me, when they know something."

"Who did all this?"

"Your benefactor is a friend of a friend. I haven't met him, but he uses his money to help people in need."

"I've been praying for someone to help us. I, mostly prayed for Doug. He was badly hurt by her. I didn't think that he would survive."

"Let me check you over, so that you can help us nurse Doug back to health."

"Sam, turn around at the next convenient spot."

"What's going on?" I started to pull into a parking lot.

"The team has completed their mission. We can head back to the store."

"What did they find?" I was getting antsy. I hoped that they found Doug and Lori.

"I won't be briefed on the situation until later. When I know something, I'll let you know." The drive back was very quiet. Both of us were lost in our own thoughts. I didn't even ask if Pat was still following us. It seemed that most of the problems have been left to the professionals.

The parking lot was about half full. I parked the T-Bird back in her spot. Heading into the store, I noticed that Tim had already made his exit. Not only was he a guitar god, but a man of mystery, too!

Linda spotted me as I walked through the door. "I'm glad you're back. Father Eugene and Andy have been waiting for you."

"Did they say what they wanted? Where are they?"

"No, they didn't say. They are in your office."

"Okay, I'll take care of them first, thanks."

"Afternoon, sorry to keep you waiting. What can I do for you?"

"It's about Patricia Jones. She has someone in the national office on her side or in her pocket. Jim Connally is supposed to look into how badly she has been treated by the people out here, especially by you." Father looked worried. Andy seemed angry.

"I know it won't help, but the national office can shove Pat Jones up their asses. She is the main suspect in two missing person cases, along with the ongoing harassment against me. I'm sorry, but you won't get any cooperation from me. Soon, I hope to be able to give you the reason why."

"Christ, Sam. do you always have to do it the hard way? These people mean business."

"When this is done, they may not have any business at all. Tell them that my lawyer will be contacting them. That is the last thing that I'm going to say on the matter."

"Okay, we'll leave it at that." My friends or soon to be ex-friends left my office. I looked up a number and called it.

"Tavin Long, attorney. How can I help you?"

"Tavin, Sam Simone. I need a favor from you."

"Let me hear what's going on." I gave him all of the details that I knew. He agreed to send them a back-off letter that would leave them scorched. I knew that he would come through for me. I saved his woman and his butt. I know that he is a good lawyer and a good man. I hoped that solved the problem.

I went out to see how the day was going in the store. I was feeling better about Doug and Lori, even without the details, plus I think that I poked Pat with my response to her bullshit.

My first place that I checked out was the new appliance trainers. Standing in the doorway to the shop, I found the room full of store ready appliances. Joe was working with Joey on some repairs.

"I didn't see you standing there. How long have you been there?"

"Just long enough to see that I asked the right person to help us out. You're pretty good at this. No wonder your stores do so well."

"Thanks for the complement. Joey is a natural. He's done most of the work. He's done it right, too!" Two days in a roll. My kids have been complemented. Jude and I must be doing something right.

THE CRAZY WOMAN OF GOOD SAMS

Pat was freaked out by the weird trip that Sam had taken her on. She was lucky that no cops saw her erratic driving on the way to her hideaway. Pat turned down her secluded driveway. She didn't notice a van hidden behind some trees. Her visitors had left enough surveillance equipment to track every move and sound that she made. By the time that she had parked her car in the garage, she was ready to take care of her prisoners.

She tossed her coat and purse on a chair in the living room. That's when she noticed that the house seemed different. Hustling to the room. At first, she felt relief, the door was closed. When she opened the door, the room was empty. Lori couldn't have carried Doug out, even if she had found a way to open the door. Rage overwhelmed her. Pat started smashing things. Screaming her rage out. After her outburst, she collapsed on the floor and slept.

Tim was waiting for me as I drove into Good Sam's the next morning. I wasn't sure how to interpret this, so I tried to keep an open mind. We walked into the store without a word spoken.

"Let me have what you've got."

"Well, Hoss, the operation was successful in removing the hostages. They were taken to a private clinic for treatment. Doug is in pretty bad shape; the medical people are not sure of his survival. Lori is in fair condition."

"Okay, what bout Pat?" Tim set up a laptop before he continued. "I think that you need to watch what we recorded after Pat came back." The recording was very clear. Pat had an epic meltdown. She screamed incoherently throughout her sickening smashing of the room. My name spewed out of her mouth numerous times as this horrendous scene played out.

"That is one scary person."

"My men believe that you will be her main target now. I have approved their plan to keep you in one piece while setting Pat up for a big fall."

"Tell me, how do you have this organization at your fingertips?"

"Sam, I made a lot of money during my Rock Star days. A lot of money. I didn't spend any money when I was still playing, but when Shelley disappeared, I spent my money on looking for her. After hiring some inept companies, I decided to form my own company. They only had two directives, find Shelley and keep me out of sight. I also invested in some other businesses, like the Big A, that have given me a good income. I guess that you could say that I'm rich. The only thing is that us guys from the "Pig Hill" don't need much in the way of material things. You should know that."

"I do know that. You really have been watching over me and Jody all of this time."

"I take care of my friends. Jody helps out people on the downside, plus she's a sucker for helping old people. You give to so many people every day. I bet that you don't how many people that you touch. Your players, your customers, your children all have received your touch. I watched all of this and decided to become a real person, not a Rock-God."

"Thank you, I love you, brother." I hugged my friend with a mist in my eyes.

Pat opened her eyes. Every inch of her hurt. She wasn't sure how long she had been out on the hard floor. It must have been a while. Nothing in the room was in one piece. She had never felt rage like the rage that had exploded from her. Her episodes were getting worse. She had almost lost control over herself when the rage came on. Her prisoners were gone, the room wrecked and she knew that her plans were ruined, too! It was only a matter of time before they came for her. She got up to work out her escape.

Dr. Brady was in early to make her rounds. She stopped at the nurse's station to look at her patient's charts. Nothing was out of the ordinary, so she started her rounds. Lori was awake when Dr. Brady came into her room.

"Good morning, Lori, how are you doing this morning?"

"I'm feeling a whole lot better. I'd feel even better if I could see Doug or at least know that he is okay."

"You can't see him just yet, but he is stable for now. He has a long way to go before we will know his outcome."

"Have they caught her yet?"

"Not that I've heard, but these people will work till they do. Let me take a look at you, before I move on to the next patient." The doctor did a thorough exam before leaving with a smile.

Today was a sales day. The store was overflowing with customers. A man walked in and stood looking around. The man didn't standout in any way, just an average looking man. Linda approached the man. "Can I help you with anything?"

"Yes, I'd like to talk to your manager."

"That would be me."

"No, I'm was told that the manager was a man."

"The store director is a man, but I'm the manager."
The man was starting to sweat. Linda decided to get Sam to
find out what is the man's problem. "Wait here, I'll get Mr.
Simone."

"Sam, I think we have a problem by the door."

"Okay, let's see what is going on." They walked back
to the man.

"I'm Sam Simone, how can I help you?" Sam extended
his hand toward the very nervous man.

"Can we talk in private?"

"Sure, let's go into my office. Linda, lead the way."

Once in the office, the man relaxed a little.

"I'm Brian Sanderson, the Executive Director of Stores
for the National Good Samaritan Society."

"Why are you here? My lawyer has talked to the
National office and they agreed to back-off. If this has to do
with Patricia Jones. You need to talk to your law
department."

"What do you mean that they agreed to back-off? Our
investigation has barely started. We believe that this region
and especially you have caused her to lose her job."

"Mr. Sanderson, make a call to your office and see if what I told you is true. You came out here without an ounce of information about the situation. No one from your office is supposed to make contact with me about Ms. Jones. Go ahead and call." I gave him the office phone. He had a one-sided conversation with someone back East. His face turned many different colors before he ended his call.

"None of this sounds like the Pat that I know. The person that I called wouldn't lie. I'm sorry, I let my feelings for Pat dismiss my good sense. I may lose my job over this. I've been advised to return at once. When she told me about coming to check out a problem manager, I believed her. She has done some fine work since she's been in my office. I put my job and marriage in jeopardy over her." Mr. Sanderson broke down in tears. Linda and I gave him some time to compose himself. He finally stood up and walked stiffly out the door.

"I don't know what Pat does, but it's scary. I hope they go easy on that poor guy." Linda had a perplexed look as she spoke. I was heading to my office when I heard a loud squeal and a bang. Looking out the front window, I saw a car backing up and pealing out. A person was on the ground.

"Call 911. Somebody just got hit. I'm going out to check on them." I ran across the lot. The victim looked like a man. As I got closer, I realized it was Brian Sanderson. I bent over to see if he was conscious. It was too late. The driver had run him over before fleeing the scene. A crowd was gathering. A man was coming towards me.

"Are you Sam Simone?" I nodded to the man. "The person that hit him was Patricia Jones."

"How do you know that?"

"I work for Tim. We have all of it on our surveillance camera. When the police show up, I'll give them a copy. Could you call Tim?"

"Yes, I'll call him right now. Is anyone following Pat?"

"Yes, Mr. Simone, we have enough operatives to handle just about any situation. Do you know who the man is?"

"I just met him. He worked with Patricia in the Good Samaritan National office."

"I'm pretty sure that he is the man she has been talking to over the last few weeks. They had some type of relationship."

"I wonder how many more dead or missing people had a relationship with her?" The operative went back to his car. I phoned Tim.

"Hey Sam, what's up?"

"There has been an accident. Pat ran over a man from the Good Sam's national office. One of your operatives asked me to call you. The police are on the way."

"Is the man dead?"

"Yes."

"I'll be right there."

The police and medical units showed up. They were quick to push back the crowd. I waited until they came over to me, before telling them what had happened. Tim arrived. He began consulting his man. After talking to his operative, Tim made his way to the investigating officers.

"I need to relay some information about the hit and run driver."

"Who are you? Did you witness the accident?"

"My name is Timothy Tobegan. I didn't witness the hit and run, but my employee witnessed it and has it all on video. Sgt. Dargey and Officer McBee have been investigating a number of incidents involving a Patricia Jones. Call them and see if you want to view our tape and other evidence that we've acquired."

"You're that rock guy, what type of company are you talking about?"

"It's a security company. So, you make the call, but remember that Ms. Jones has made threats against Mr. Simone. My company is working to keep her from following through on her threats."

"Who is the dead guy on the ground?"

"I don't know, but I know that he had just talked with Mr. Simone. Ask him." Tim made his way back to me.

"Hopefully, they'll call Dargey. I think it is time to lay our cards down. The police need to be involved with the rest of the show."

"If the police decide to believe us and get involved. What happens next?"

"It's hard to tell. If Pat decides to run or if she is that over the edge, we get completely different endings."

While we were talking, Sgt. Dargey arrived. He appeared in front of us. "The investigating officer told me that you might be able to identify the victim."

"His name is Brian Sanderson. He worked for the National Good Samaritan office. He came to the store this morning, claiming that he was here to investigate me for my treatment of Patricia Jones. It turns out that he came on an unofficial basis. I set him straight on the Society backing out of the problem after my lawyer's contacting them. He left on a sad note, fearing that he had ruined his career and marriage over his involvement with Ms. Jones. Less than a minute after leaving there was a loud screech and boom. I saw a car leaving the scene in a hurry. By the time that I ran to the victim; he was dead."

"Sam, what is this about witnesses and video?"

"Well, Sgt. You'll have to talk to Mr. Tobegan. I'm sure that he can give you all of that information."

It was over an hour before customers were allowed to leave or come into the store. Tim made his way inside around this time. We went into my office to talk.

"What is going to happen now?"

"Well Hoss, it got more complicated as I was talking to the officers. It seems that Pat hit two more cars as she tried to get away, both accidents had injuries. The scene of the second accident was pretty bad. My guys stopped to give aid to the injured. We lost contact at that point. Our hope is that she returns to her house. That is a slim hope. I've set up a meeting with the Auburn Police. Men will be deployed at Good Sam's and your house. Right now, I have to go to the meeting."

"Let's hope that you and the police get a break. She needs to be stopped. I would like to visit Doug and Lori, if it can be arranged."

"I'll talk to you after the meeting." Tim headed to the meeting. I stood there for a while before I went back into the store. A few of the customers asked me if the guy that got hit was the same man that was just in the store. I told them what I could, but I kept moving to try and clear my head.

Pat had driven so long that she didn't know where she was. When she saw Brian get out of the car at Good Sam's she had pulled closer. Her mind was racing about what to do. As she saw Brian talking to Sam through the front window. A live Brian would just complicate things. Everything was too complicated as it was. Watching Brian walk out to his car, forced her decision. Pat revved the engine and ran him over. He flipped over her car and landed with an ugly thump. After that, Pat didn't remember much of what she did, except that she drove really fast. She finally slowed down, before pulling off the road. Her whole body was shaking. It took a long time to settle her nerves enough to even begin thinking about what was needed to do now.

The police had been able to get a search warrant based on the evidence that Tim and his company had provided. They executed a search. The search provided more backup to what was already known. Now, the hard part would be finding Patricia Jones. The police were also searching Doug and Lori's properties finding evidence of the abductions.

I went home after the long horrible day. I sat down on the couch, drained from all of the events, of the day. A knock at the door brought me out of my mist.

"Hoss, I know that you've had a really bad day, even for you, but this is the first chance that I've had to talk to you about Doug and Lori. Doug is not doing very well. He may have some permanent health issues. Lori on the other is doing fine. Like I told you before, they are in a private clinic. I can guarantee that they are safe. Now with Pat still on the loose, I can't take you to the clinic. It would be too dangerous for all of you. The clinic is secure, but you're not."

"Is this clinic yours?"

"I'm one of the owners. We set it up for people that needed to be safe. Once I began to change the way I lived my life, I put my money and time into a lot of different businesses and people. Each of these enterprises gives back to people in need. I like to think of it as Good Sam's on a larger scale."

"You are amazing. Is Jody involved in all of this?"

"No. She knows about them, but her contribution is more important than all of those. She gave me a family. You remember how much time that I spent at your house. I have been looking for that ever since. My wife and child are the most important things in my life. I used to be jealous of you. I didn't understand how you had never gone anyplace, but found such a good life. I stopped chasing that and let it find me."

"I'm glad that you found Jody and Samantha. I couldn't tell you how great it was to finally find Jude and David to finish my family. The whole story wasn't all good. My parents are gone and I'm not close to my siblings. You met Jane, so what I'm saying is that you just have to keep living every day. We all search for some form of happiness. Here's to finding Pat and closing this horribly bad chapter."

CLOSING THE BAD CHAPTER

Pat was hidden from the road. She got out of her car. Popping the trunk open. Quickly, changing the plates on the car. A fast survey of the damage to the car surprised her. The car showed little or no damage. A few minor scrapes were all that she found. New plates would give her some more time to figure out her next move. Soon, she was back on the road. The rage was receding. A small motel was pleased to get cash for her stay. Sleep hit her as soon as she settled into the shabby little room.

"Sam, I'm worried about this crazy woman coming here. Are you sure that Tim's company can keep all of us safe?"

"Honey, I don't know, but I'm willing to trust Tim. It seems that everybody is looking for her. With a little luck, someone will find her. What have the kids said about it?"

"None of them are freaking out, they seem to want to just keep doing what they're doing. I'm worried about you, mostly."

"I'm worried about me. This is the weirdest of the weird. A few months ago, I didn't know any of these people., now I'm the center of this crazy woman's universe."

With input from my friends and family, I decided to try to act as normal possible. That was one way to show that I wasn't giving into Pat's crazy mind. With all of this in mind, I decided to take Marie out for practice in her car. I hadn't spent much time with Marie on her driving. The date for her driver's test was fast approaching. Marie was waiting for me in her Elantra. We went over everything that she needed to do before we backed out and did our thing. Marie had clearly paid attention to the driver's course. She was spot on. She had the driving down very well for a new driver. I let her choose where we were going. She drove to Twin Rivers and back. I think that she was ready for the test. I hope that her driving was this good when she took the test.

"Thanks, Dad. I didn't feel nervous at all. You were great, just letting me drive. I remember when Joey was learning, he told me that you scared the crap out of him when he was driving."

"That was three years ago. I was a rookie at helping my kid learn to drive. If I had to do it over again, I would."

"Maybe, it isn't too bad sometimes being the younger child. Thanks again." We headed into the house on a good note.

"You told Sam about some of your enterprises, that's great. You certainly aren't a typical millionaire."

"I'm not a typical anything, but I know that I love you and Samantha way above typical."

"Give me a kiss, Rock-Star." Tim obliged Jody. He was still very concerned about keeping Sam safe. Sam was a big boy, but this was an odd situation. Crazy people were usually loose-cannons, making it hard to figure their patterns out. After his family, Tim cared about his old friend the most.

Sgt. Dargey was working late. His desk was piled high with cases. The case that worried him the most was the Patricia Jones case. The evidence they had gathered built a strong case against her, but if they couldn't find her it would all be for naught. As he went through the mess on his desk, he put aside everything that was connected with the case. One of the last papers he looked at was about a car seen at a motel. The plates were different, but the car was driven by a woman did fit. He'd check out the motel in the morning.

Doug woke up after many days in the clinic. He was still unable to speak, but he responded to the nurses.

"Dr. Brady, this is Helen from the clinic. You left orders to call when we had any changes in Doug Toms. He woke up. He is still unable to speak, but he responded to the nurses."

"That's encouraging news, thank you for the call. I'll be in at the start of day shift."

Dr. Brady showed up at 6:30. She grabbed a coffee from the lounge. After, settling into a chair in the corner, she began looking at patient notes. The notes on Doug Toms jumped off the pages at her. She had feared that Mr. Toms was losing his battle, but his waking up last night gave her and him new hope.

"Dr. Brady, Tim Tobegan is on the phone. He would like to speak to you."

"Tell him that I'll be right there." She got up and began making her way to the nurse's station. The nurse pointed at line one.

"Hello, this is Dr. Brady."

"Good morning, this is Tim Tobegan. Do you have a minute?"

"Sure, it's early, so I'm just looking over the night charts. What's on your mind?"

"I would like to know when it will be possible for Lori Smalls and Doug Toms to have visitors?"

"Well, Ms. Smalls is ready for company, but Doug Toms has just regained consciousness. Is this in your official capacity as the director of the clinic?"

"No, it is not in any way official. Mr. Toms' boss has asked to check on the patients. I told him that I would keep an eye on how they were doing, but it might not be feasible to arrange a visit. There is still a danger from the woman that abducted them."

"Why don't we give it a few more days. Some of the loose ends may get cleared up. I'll keep you informed."

"Thank you for your time, Doctor. You are always a pleasure to talk to."

The Simone house was awake. The house was filled with the family getting ready for their day. David was singing a loud, happy song while he ate his breakfast. Joey and Marie were hustling around trying to get out the door without forgetting anything. Marie had a game tonight, Joey had classes and work. I was stumbling along clearing my mind after a short shower. Jude was working her magic on David. She would drop David off at school before heading to work. I was usually the last to leave in the morning.

"Dad, it's a home game at 3:30."

"I'll be there. Jude are you going to the game?"

"Not today, I have a meeting. You need to pick David up at school. Okay?"

"I'll be there, maybe even on time."

"Daddio, don't forget me like that one time." David laughed. Jeez, forget a kid once and you never hear the end of it.

As I was sitting at my desk looking over sales figures, I felt like I had been on vacation. Everything seemed to jump out at me. My mind had been elsewhere for a few weeks, but looking at the stores sales I was a complete blank. The numbers were good, so good that I should have given the crew a "Good Job". If I could fix anything, that I seemed to have missed, this is it. I buzzed for Linda to come to my office and waited.

"What's up, Bossman?"

"Come in and grab a seat. Have you seen the sales reports for the last few weeks?"

"No, I was waiting for you. Your mind has been else where the last few weeks."

"That thought just reached up and smacked me in the face. I apologize for being out of it. These numbers really did smack me in the face. They're that good. Look at these numbers." I handed Linda the reports. She quietly read them, before looking up and grinning at me.

"You're right, Sam, that is one of the best sales reports that I've seen in all the years I've been here."

"I think that we need to celebrate, so pizza is on Good Sam's. Set up pizza days for all three stores. Same as we always do it. And Linda, I apologize for being in such a dense fog, but with your leadership we can weather anything." I spent the rest of the day catching up on what I spaced off the last few weeks.

THE CRAP HITS THE FAN

The Simone's came home from Marie's game with smiles on their faces. Twin Rivers won again. The team looked good, very good. Every part of their game was hitting on all cylinders. This was a better team than last year's playoff team. Marie was having a darn good season, so far. She was driving her teammates to be better. This new coach was allowing them to play, after the Cummings years of tirades and boneheaded coaching it felt like I, for the first time, could just watch and enjoy them playing.

I woke up refreshed. I was eager to go to work. The Pat thing was still there, but it had moved aside just a bit. Part of that was Doug and Lori being safe. I wasn't as worried about myself. Tim and his security guys gave me a small sense of safety.

The Auburn Police were setting up a couple of detectives to go with Sgt. Dargey and Officer McBee to check out a motel where a car and woman matching the descriptions of Pat Jones had been reported.

"Wetzl and Peterson will cover the exits at the motel. So, far she has never shown any weapons. If she tries to run, you guys will try to stop her. We need to get her off the streets in one piece. Any questions?"

"Sarge, how sure are we?"

"Not one-hundred percent, but my gut tells me it's her." The men headed out to their cars. Twenty minutes later they pulled into the motel. Dargey and McBee got out. They made a quick stop in the office. The manager said that the suspect was in Room 16. Quietly, the officers made their way to room 16. Just as they were knocking on the door, a loud noise came from behind them. Pat Jones had dropped her package and ran to her car. The officer's chased her. She was inside the now running car.

"Stop, put your hands up!"

She slammed back and began to leave the parking lot. The officers fired at the car. Hitting it multiple times. Pat just kept going. The car smacked the squad car at the exit from the motel. The car was damaged beyond use. Dargey and McBee were now in their car and in pursuit.

"Officers in pursuit on Military Road south."

They gave dispatch as much info as they had. Try as they could, she was outpacing them.

"She drives like a madman or woman. I can hardly see her now."

"We'll keep our pursuit until we can't see her anymore." The men soon lost her in traffic.

"Our day has just gone from bad to worse. I have no idea how we're going to flush her out now."

"Well, Sarge, I think that our best bet will be her anger at Sam Simone. If we concentrate on him, we might get her."

"You might be right. Now I guess that we'll head back in and start our paperwork. And of course, our ass-chewing." Both men laughed.

Pat was frantically looking for a place to lay low for a while. As she drove, her thoughts ran through her head. It was like watching a coming attractions clip over and over at the theater. Nothing that she saw helped her. The craziness seemed to pile on and overwhelm her. She needed a chance to rest. Without her even being aware, she pulled into an overgrown lot. The house didn't look livable, but she could hide the car behind it and maybe get some rest. As soon as she felt secure, she went to sleep.

"Good Samaritan's, how can I help you?"

"Sam, this is Joe Johnson. I wanted to call you early enough to let you that I won't be able to make it tomorrow for the appliance lesson. An emergency came up. I'm sorry."

"Don't worry about it. You're doing us a favor. I'm giving the employees a pizza party for the good job they've been doing. The pizza party starts about the time that you would be starting, so one day off won't matter too much."

"Thanks Sam, we'll be there for the next lesson."

Just as I finished my phone call, someone knocked on my door.

"Come in."

Sgt. Dargey made his entrance, looking a little sheepish.

"Sam, do you have a minute?"

"Sure, have a seat. What can I do for you today?"

"I'm feeling a little foolish about what I need to tell you, but here goes. This morning we went to check on a lead about Pat Jones. I'm still kicking myself over the outcome. It was a good lead. We had backup and were ready for her, or so we thought. She went through us like a greased pig. We lost her in traffic. I don't know where she is, but we think that she'll come after you. I believe that she'll come after you at the store."

"First off, stop kicking yourself. This is one crazy, but smart individual. She has fooled a lot of people for a long time. Sarge, I really think that you'll get her. Tell me what you want me to do and I'll do it."

Patricia woke up in her car. She was foggy-headed. As she looked around, she wasn't sure where she was and how she got there. A blurry scene flashed into her mind. Her head started clearing. Somehow, the police had found her, but she was able to get away. She must have driven a long way. Nothing around her looked familiar. All that she knew was that she was cold, hungry, and bent on finding someone to take her anger out on. Simone was the only one left that would feed her anger. Patricia opened the door and stepped out to stretch her legs and pee. It was still early dawn. The car started up and Pat headed out to feed her anger.

I woke up to the sounds of my family. After, a quick shower, I headed towards the kitchen. The smell of food was calling me, but I also needed to tell Joey about the trainer cancelling this morning. As usual, I was the last to join the morning madness.

"Joey, Joe Johnson called yesterday to tell me that he wouldn't be in today. Something came up. He'll be there tomorrow."

"In that case, I may not come in, either. It depends on my other classes. I can use some library time for them."

"That's alright, we're having a pizza party for the employees. Not much gets done on pizza day."

"Daddio, can I skip school for pizza day?"

"I don't think so, little man."

"Dad, remember I have a game tomorrow. We're playing Alpac." Marie added.

"I have it on my schedule."

I looked towards Jude; she had a troubled look on her face. I wasn't sure if I should ask. Sometimes, my intuition is way off when it comes to my wife. I guess that's never stopped me before, so here goes.

"Honey, is everything okay?"

"Yeah, no, I'm not sure. I had some odd dreams that woke me up, but I couldn't see them clearly. I'm sure that they're nothing."

Now, I was more concerned than when I started. Jude seemed really spooked by her dreams. I didn't push it any further.

"I love you," was my lame reassurance. We all headed out to meet our days.

Pat bought an extra-large coffee at a convenience store. As the caffeine kicked in, she began formulating a plan. She was very jittery when she crossed the line into Auburn. The combination of coffee and her recent escape from the police caused tingling through her whole body. She passed The Good Samaritan Store before turning on the next block. Finding a parking lot that bordered the back of Good Sam's. She hid her car behind a storage shed in the lot. Taking a few items from the trunk, she made her way to the fence around the back side of the store. It wasn't dawn yet, so she was able to cut her way through the fence, before heading to the back of the store. Looking around she spotted a place to conceal herself. Waiting and watching until the employees arrived.

I was busy setting up the store. I had an overwhelming need to be busy. Today was the pizza party. Most of the employees are on the schedule to work today. Both trucks would get an early start, so they could be back in time for the food. There was a buzz of workers scurrying in and out of the store with new merchandise. As it got closer to opening, I glanced around, everything looked clean. The store was overflowing with merchandise. Linda unlocked the front door while turning the signs around to signal the start of our day. A large crowd of customers flowed in. We were slammed for the first half of the day.

Around noon, Linda asked if I'd watch for the pizza guy. I agreed, because watching for the pizza guy is one of my specialties. It wasn't a long wait. The pizzas and other goodies were soon headed to the breakroom. Linda and Bob would set up the party for the employees. I sent Angela to help them. Leaving me to watch the store.

"I love to come in when you're out in the store. How are you today?"

"I'm doing fine. How are you doing Mrs. Dantone?"

"Just great. I came in to pick up some voucher requests, so I thought I'd get some shopping in. The store looks good. Tell Linda that I think she's doing a great job as the manager."

Mrs. Dantone gave me a wink and a smile as she went out the door.

The breakroom was ready for the employees. The food smelled wonderful. I usually ordered pizza from *Rome's Best Pizza*. They have never disappointed me. Bob went out to tell the warehouse employees that the pizza party was ready. The trucks pulled up to the loading area as Bob made his announcement. The whole crew was in the breakroom, except me. I was the only employee in the store. I would make my way over later.

Pat had spent the morning watching. She was well hidden, so nobody noticed her. Something seemed to be going on. She saw the pizza delivery man, followed by the trucks coming in and the two store employees going into the warehouse. The only no-show was Sam. He had to be in the store. The customer traffic had slowed to a crawl. Her first impulse was to make her move now. She acted on it by exiting her hiding spot. Carefully, she scanned the area. Nobody was in sight. It was now or never, but never wasn't a choice that she could make. Slowly, entering the store from the side door, she saw that Sam was checking out the only customer she could see. Pat slipped behind a large refrigerator, she waited. The transaction was soon finished.

After finishing with the last customer, I went out to the clothes racks in front of the cash register. It was my first chance to straighten out the morning's mess. The first thing that needed to be done was rehanging clothes. One eye watched the front door for more customers. Just as I bent over to pick up some clothes, I felt something or someone behind me. Turning to see if they needed some help. I faced Pat holding a nasty looking knife.

"Hello Sam, how are you doing today?" Pat had a bright smile on her face.

"It was a pretty good day, until you showed up."

"Walk outside. I don't want to make a mess in the store."

"That's really nice of you."

"God, I hate you. You ruined all of my plans. The least that you can do is die."

"I'll tell you this, I'm not going easy."

I was stalling for time. Pat's hands were shaking. I, having never faced a crazy person with a knife, I was feeling a little shaky myself. I heard the door open.

"Store's closed," I yelled to the unknown person.

Linda ran back to the warehouse. She was fumbling with her cell-phone. "We need help at Good Sam's. A woman with a knife is holding Sam in the store."

The phone call stopped everyone in their tracks. The employees started to move towards the store.

"Everybody, sit down. The police are coming. Bob, Leon, and Dave sneak around and cover the front door. I'm going back to side door. The rest of you sit down and wait until the situation is under control."

Linda found some steel that she didn't know that she had.

The guys were soon out front. Linda was at the side door. Linda desperately, tried to signal Sam. She wasn't sure that he saw the signal. He had.

I could see that Pat was fully focused on me. We had moved closer to the front door. I saw the guys out front and Linda at the side door. I didn't want to draw them into this situation, so I figured that I would make my move as we went through the door.

The policed hadn't showed up when we started through the door. It was time to end this. I side stepped while turning towards Pat. She reacted by slicing at me. I felt a stinging, burning pain as we tumbled to the ground. My left side was bleeding as I rolled off of Pat, that's the last thing that I remember.

Linda and the guys rushed to me. The police were arriving.

"She has a knife. Sam's been wounded."

"You come over with me. The rest of you stand back."

The police soon discovered that Pat had somehow fallen on her knife. Paramedics began working on Sam.

"Is she dead?"

"Yes, it looks like she landed on her knife."

"Geez, I'm glad. I know that isn't very nice, but I really am glad that this is over."

"What do you mean over?"

"That is Patricia Jones. She's wanted for abducting Doug Toms and Lori Smalls, plus killing Brian Sanderson. She may even be wanted for more. She has been threatening Sam through all of this."

"I need your name and to ask you a few questions."

Before I could answer, Sgt. Dargey and Officer McBee appeared.

"Continue with what you're doing. We're here because she is at the heart of our investigation. I want to hear what happened today, so I'll just listen. McBee, would you check on our two victims and talk to those employees that witnessed the assault."

Father Eugene, Al, and Andy showed up. Father bent over where the paramedics were working on Sam. He said a prayer before turning to Pat's lifeless body. He prayed the last rites for her. The paramedics were ready to transport Sam to the hospital. Linda squeezed Sam's hand and kissed his forehead. She was crying as they took him away.

Linda was huddled with Father Eugene, Andy, and Al. They were discussing what happened. Sgt. Dargey approached them.

"Is there a place where the employees could go to so that we could start interviewing witnesses?"

"The employee breakroom should work for what you need."

"Thanks, Father. We are closing access to the store. It will only be a few more minutes before we start the interviews. I'll try to let the employees leave as soon as we have enough of our work done. Fatalities take a lot of work."

The Good Sam employees and board started towards the breakroom. There was a lot of police working around the silent remains of Pat Jones. The store property was being searched by more officers.

"Linda, would you call Sam's wife?"

"I'm calling right now."

Linda called more than Jude. She also called Tim. Tim and Jody would call Josephine, Charley, Mac, and any other friends that they could think of.

The ambulance hadn't gone a block before Sam woke up struggling against his restraints.

"Calm down, Mr. Simone. You've been injured. We're taking you to the hospital."

I looked around. I was in the back of the aid unit. The pain wasn't as bad as it felt before. I guess that Pat must have stabbed or cut me when we went out the door.

"What happened to Pat?"

"Is Pat the woman that attacked you?"

"Yes, the last thing that I remember was struggling to get the knife away from her."

"She didn't make it."

"I'm sorry, she was very troubled. Did anyone else get hurt?"

"As far as we know, there was only two injuries. Try to relax. We'll be at the hospital in a few minutes."

"Sarge, we found her car. It was in a lot behind the store on the next block. It looks like she cut through the fence to gain access."

PICKING UP THE PIECES

McBee and Dargey made their way into the employee breakroom at Good Sam's. The room was filled with worried employees. A muffled noise filled the area. People were praying and talking. Many had called their families to let them know that they were okay. Father Eugene had circled the room helping anyone that needed an encouraging word. Andy and Al sat with Linda, holding her hand as she cried.

"Hello, I'm Sgt. Dargey and this is Officer McBee. We will try to ask our questions and let you all go home as fast as we can."

The officers began talking to the employees. The process took a little over two hours. The information that was gleaned from the group would fill in the blanks. Hopefully, this would give them a way to close the file on Patricia Jones.

"Linda, I think that you can let your people go home. We are done with our investigation, so you can start closing and securing the store."

"Thank you, Sarge. Have you had any word on Sam?"

"Nothing, except that he's in the emergency room waiting for surgery."

Jude had contacted the kids. Giving them the little information that she had. Jude rushed to pick up David from school. Marie and Joey met her in the parking lot of the hospital. Marie started crying as soon as she saw Jude. Joey was crying as he wrapped his arms around his sister. The Simone's walked into the hospital as one.

"I need to find Sam Simone."

"Are you family?"

"I'm his wife and these are our kids."

"I'll get someone to take you to him."

They didn't have a very long wait. It still seemed like an eternity. The family was lost in thoughts, prayers, and anxiety while time went on. A nurse came to them. She quietly took them to see him.

I was awake when my world walked through the door. The pain went away for a few moments as I saw their tear stained faces.

"Sam, how are you doing?"

"Dad, I love you."

"Daddio, please get better."

"I'm sorry that I wasn't there to help you."

"I love all of you. The doctors tell me that they need to repair some damage to my shoulder. The surgery won't take too long. If all goes right, I'll be home tomorrow.

Jude, talk to the desk for where the surgical waiting room is. I'm going to be fine."

The family kissed me and headed to the desk. I was ready to go. A team rolled me out of the emergency room towards the elevator.

Just as Jude was finishing at the desk, a crowd of friends and family came into the waiting room. The nurse's eyes bulged when she saw how many people were now standing with the Simone's. This man was certainly loved by a lot of people. A priest stepped up to the counter.

"As you can see, there are a lot of people here for Mr. Simone. Is the waiting room large enough to accommodate everyone?"

"You're Father Eugene from Blessed Family?"

"Yes, Sam is a friend of mine and all of these people."

"I think that the chapel next to the surgical waiting room would hold all of you and maybe some more, too!"

The throng moved to the elevators. It took a few trips to get everyone upstairs. The large group was settled in the chapel. Father Eugene started the Rosary. Most of the group joined in. The leaders of the Good Samaritan Society decided to get some refreshments for the people. Most of them hadn't eaten since lunch.

"Father, something has got to be done about all of the damn people that have been trying to take a chunk out of Sam these last few years."

"I wish that I had an answer for you Josephine, but all we can do today, is hope and pray. Even if we could do something, I don't think that Sam is going to change."

Josephine let loose with her signature cackle. "You're right Father. I don't want to lose that boy. He used to give me a ride home every day. His parents raised him right."

They exploded into stories about the things that Sam had done for all of them.

"Marie, are you listening to all of the stories about Dad?"

"Yes, I didn't know about most of them. I guess that he's way more complicated than we give him credit for."

"It's hard to see beyond him being our Dad. Others see him as an adult. An adult that helps when help is needed. He's special to us, but in a dad way."

"Marie, Joey where is Dad?"

"David, Daddy has a boo-boo, a really bad boo-boo. The doctors are fixing it. Everybody is waiting to see if the doctors can fix it. David come sit on my lap."

David climbed into Marie's lap and snuggled up. He was soon fast asleep. Marie scanned the room. It was filled with friends and family from Good Sam's, Blessed Family, and soccer. The people gathered made her feel like they were blessed.

"Well, everybody, it looks like we we're just about done here. I think that the damage has been repaired. I'll go talk to the family after we get the patient settled in recovery."

Dr. Johnston headed to the nurse's station to get the family information. "Where is Mr. Simone's family?"

"You can't miss them. They are in the chapel."

He walked around the corner to the chapel. He heard them before he saw them. The chapel was overflowing with people. He carefully, made his way through the throng of well-wishers.

"Excuse me, I would like to talk to the Simone family."

"We're over here."

The doctor spotted Jude and the kids in the middle of the crowd.

"I'm Dr. Johnston. Your husband is in recovery. The surgery went well. I was able to repair the damage. He should recover full use of his shoulder. Any questions?"

"When can we see him and how long will he be in the hospital?"

"You should be able to see in an hour; a nurse will come to let you know that he's awake. Without any setbacks, he should be able to go home tomorrow."

"Thank you. I'm sure that we'll have more questions later."

"I'll be glad to answer any question that I can."

Dr. Johnston quietly slipped out of the room. The room gave a collective sigh of relief.

It seemed that I was a long way away, but I kept hearing voices. I was drawn to the voices. At first it was a struggle to reach out to them. I finally had enough awareness to answer.

"Can you hear me?"

"Yes," I squeaked out sorely.

My eyes opened to see a nurse looking back at me. She gave me some sips of water. I was beginning to focus more clearly.

"Welcome back. Your surgery went fine. The doctor will be in to see you later. As soon as you're a little more awake, we'll let your family see you. Do you need anything?"

"Something to drink, my throat's a little sore."

"That's pretty normal. There is a glass of ice chips to sip on."

The nurse helped me take a few sips. The soreness started to go away.

A nurse approached Jude in the chapel. "Mrs. Simone, your husband is awake. The kids and you can come and see him, now."

Joey carried a very tired David. Marie and Jude held hands as the group made its way to see Sam.

I looked up and saw the most spectacular sight. My family standing around my bed. Tears of joy flowed down my face. I couldn't get up, but they all touched me and cried. I kept hearing their voices giving words of love.

"You guys are the best medicine anyone could ever have."

"Sam, the doctor said that the surgery went well. He said if you don't have any setbacks, you'll be released tomorrow. You scared the crap out of us."

"Well Pat scared the crap out of me. Did the police get her?"

"Pat's dead. When she stabbed you, somehow, she ended up falling on her knife. She was dead before the police showed up."

"Dad, there is a chapel full of your friends and family."

"A chapel full, out there for me. I'm feeling blessed."

"Look, David conked out on your bed."

"I love you guys."

"Sam, I think that I'm going to take the little guy and go home. I'll find out how early we can come and get you."

Jude leaned over and kissed me, followed by Joey and Marie. I rubbed David's head before they headed home.

"I know that the crowd in the chapel can't all come into see me, but could we do something for me to see them and thank them for being here for me and my family?"

"I think that we've come up with an idea. We're going to move your bed to the doorway. The people in the chapel can come by and say hello."

"That works for me."

Soon my bed was in the doorway. People started coming by. It was along line of well-wishers. Linda had a tablet that she was putting down everyone's name on. I was glad because I would not remember all of the names without it. After everyone had a chance to wish me well, the nurses announced that I needed my rest. Reluctantly, my family and friends went home. As the nurses were pushing my bed back into the room, they were marveling over the number of well-wishers that had been there for me.

"If you don't mind, can I ask you a question?"

"I don't mind. Ask away."

"What do you do to have such a turnout?"

"Nothing special, I manage the Good Samaritan stores. Those people are family, friends from Good Sam's, or people that I've met through coaching. They are people that touch a little of everything that I do."

"You're the guy from the newspaper stories and television news."

"I guess that I've had a little publicity the last couple of years."

"A little publicity. I seemed to read or watch you on the news all the time. Nothing surprises me anymore."

I was soon fast asleep.

REPAIRING THE MESS

The medical staff woke me up very early. They checked me over with a fine-toothed comb to use an old term. I was sore from my injury, but I felt pretty good overall. The one thing that I needed was food. I hadn't eaten in a day. I didn't get even one slice of pizza before Pat showed up and finished her miserable life. The nurses must have gotten my signals. Breakfast arrived and I devoured it in a few short bites. I was ready to go home. Hopefully, I passed all the tests. I really, really wanted to go home to be with my family.

The doctor showed up around nine. He wasted no time before he said that I was fit to go home.

"Mr. Simone, you are cleared to be released. Check out will be around eleven. We've called your wife. She'll need to bring some clothes and sign some papers when she arrives."

"That's great. That will be the best medicine I can get. I want to thank all of you for the care you've given me. I'll recommend you to all my friends."

Jude and the kids showed up at ten. I had clean clothes on as we filled out the discharge papers. The doctor gave me a prescription for pain which I probably wouldn't use, but you never know. David was entertaining the people on the floor. I was smiling from ear to ear. Nobody could knock the smile from my face. I was alive and heading home with my family. I owed my guardian angel a prayer of thanks. We were finally done with all the papers. Free at last. Joey went to bring the car around.

The ride home was surprisingly quiet. I was playing what I could remember of yesterday in my mind. I still couldn't put my finger on what had pushed Pat to such a tragic ending. I was sad, but grateful for surviving her attack.

"Sam, we're home."

I woke from my thoughts, looking around at my family. A wave of relief washed over me.

"That's the nicest thing, I think, I've ever heard." We walked in the door as one. Everybody had a piece of me. I had a piece of all of them, too!

"Sam, are you tired?"

"No, I just want to sit with my family for a little bit."

We spent the day talking, laughing, and being together. By the time the day was winding down, I knew that I had to do something for the real victims, Lori and Doug. There wasn't anything to do for Pat, but Lori and Doug would need help picking up their lives. I was forming a plan. I would need some help from Tim to make the plan work.

In the morning, I felt like a new man. I headed to the kitchen for my morning shot of family. Marie was up and helping Jude with breakfast.

"I'm sorry that I missed your game, Marie."

"You didn't miss it. The other team had some problem, so the game was rescheduled for later."

"That's great. I still plan to go to all of them."

"Well, I hope so. You only have one all-time great soccer player in the family," Marie was smiling like a lunatic.

David ran into the room. "Daddio, can I sit on your lap?"

"You sure can, just be careful of my shoulder, okay?"

"Okay, Daddio."

I soon had my little whirlwind on my lap giving me love.

"Are you hungry?"

"Yes ma'am!" Food magically appeared in front of us.

"I'm leaving. See everybody later."

"Joey, are you going to Good Sam's for class?"

"Yes, dad. Joe texted me that he or one of his techs would be there."

"That's good. See you later."

"Jude, is David going to school?"

"I told him that he could stay home with you if he wanted. I've already left a message with his school."

"I was hoping that he would stay with me."

"Daddio, I am staying with you."

"Oh, I thought you chose school. What do you have planned for me today?"

"Mom said that I was to be your helper, but I guess that we could watch cartoons and play a few games." My little man had a happy look on his face. He was going to help his daddy out.

"That's a good plan."

My little man, conked out at about eleven. He was snoring next to me on the couch. My phone started making noise.

"Hello, Tim. How are you this fine morning?"

"You sound pretty good for a guy that just got cut up by a crazy woman."

"I am feeling good. My littlest one just fell asleep, snoring like a chainsaw. I'm going to live another day. Why wouldn't I be feeling good?"

"I called to ask if you might be up for a little ride in a couple of days?"

"I might be, what do you have in mind?"

"I think that its about time to go see the other victims of the crazy lady. Lori is ready to go home, but Doug will need special care. I have an idea about helping them out. I'd like to tell you what is in the works."

"I guess we were thinking the same thing about Doug and Lori. Okay, when do you want to go?"

"Tomorrow, if you are up to it and if Jude gives her blessing."

"If Jude agrees, we'll make a date."

"I want to warn you that I don't kiss on the first date."

"I see that you haven't lost the Pig Hill bad humor."

"Sarge, the autopsy report is in."

"Let me see the copy. Is there anything unusual in it?"

"I think that you should read it and judge it for yourself."

The report showed the knife wound as the cause of death, but the most interesting part was that Ms. Jones had multiple brain tumors. According to the doctors, she didn't have very long to live. The tumors were so large that they may have caused her rages.

"I see what you mean. She didn't have much control over her outbursts. I wonder if she knew about the tumors?"

"I don't think that we'll ever know for sure."

"Tavin Long, my name is Arthur Chandler. I'm the lead counsel for The Good Samaritan Society. I have a proposal in the matter of Patricia Jones and Sam Simone."

"Okay, I'm listening."

"We would like to offer a settlement to Mr. Simone for his injuries. This would cover his medical bills, pain, suffering, and the harm to his family. If you accept our settlement, your client would agree to not file suit against our organization. I have faxed the documents to your office. Please read them over and get back to me with any questions. I hope that we can come to some agreement."

"I will look the settlement over. Thank you for your promptness in this matter."

Tavin spent a few minutes reading the settlement offer. Tavin sent a message with a few questions and a couple of counter measures. The back and forth went on for a couple of days before they came to an agreement. Tavin would present the agreement to Sam.

Lori was excited. Her parents were coming to visit with her son. It had been a long time since she had seen her parents and son.

"You're looking very nice. When are your mom and dad coming?"

"Lunchtime, I can hardly sit still. I'm so happy to see them. I hope that I can get out of here soon. I wish that Doug was doing better."

"Doug is physically healed, but he'll need a lot of therapy to have any chance of a normal life. I need to tell you that Mr. Tobegan will be here tomorrow to check on you and Doug."

"Who is Mr. Tobegan?"

"He is the man that owns this clinic. He also was responsible for finding you and Doug."

"I feel special. Visitors, two days in a row."

"How did your day go?"

"David entertained me until he fell asleep. My pain level was way down. Tim called. He asked if he could take me to the clinic to visit Doug and Lori, but only if you gave your blessing."

"When does he want to do this?"

"Tomorrow, if I'm up to it and you give your blessing."

Jude sat for a time in silence. She didn't say no right away, just mute contemplation.

"Are you really feeling better?"

"Yes, but I don't know what I'll feel like tomorrow."

"I trust Tim to take care of you, but you can't blame me for being hesitant. We could have lost you. I'm going to give this outing my blessing because I believe that those two need some support to help them recover. I won't even tell you to be careful. I know that you'll do the best that you can." She leaned over and kissed me. God, I love her.

The next morning, Tim showed up early. He wanted to make sure that Jude was on board our field trip. We were all seated around the table eating breakfast when Tim cleared his throat, "Jude, I want to make sure that you're okay with Sam going to the clinic today."

"I'm okay with you taking Sam to visit Lori and Doug, but my worry is about Sam over doing it. The doctor didn't put many restrictions on him. It's just that its only two days since his surgery. If anything happens, remember, I know where you live."

"I can live with that. Jude, you know that I wouldn't let anything happen to my brother of another mother."

Jude smiled. She touched Tim's hand. I think my wife likes my friend.

We got into Jody's Challenger to start our trip. So far, I felt pretty good. My shoulder hurt occasionally, but not enough to slow me down. I have no idea where this clinic is. Tim had us heading towards the Enumclaw Plateau. He took a left onto S.E. 400th.

"Tim, I feel that I need to do something to help Doug and Lori's recovery, especially Doug. I just don't know what. I don't have very much money. I do hope to figure something out."

"Hoss, that's what this visit is about. I know how you think about people needing help, so my foundation is going to make a donation to them. I want you to coordinate what to do with the money. I think that once you see Doug, you'll see that he needs lots of therapy. You will also see that Lori wants to be in his life. After this visit, we'll talk about what they need. Then we'll make it possible."

"You surprise me every time we talk. That is a generous idea that will help all of them."

I sat thinking about the direction that Tim had grown since he came back into my life.

HELPING THE NEEDY

We were driving through farmlands. The farmland was slowly losing to subdivisions, but it was still a beautiful drive. Tim slowed down to make a left onto a long driveway. I didn't see anything that looked like a clinic. The driveway went through some trees. As we drove out of the trees, I spotted the buildings. We stopped at the guard shack.

"Good morning, Mr. Tobegan, pull right in and park in the garage."

"Thank you, Georgy."

After parking the car. We walked through a covered walkway into the clinic. The place was bright and new. It looked like any large medical center. Tim knew the way, so I just followed his lead.

"Doug and Lori are on the third floor. The clinic can handle most medical issues. We see a lot of people that are willing to pay for privacy, but we also treat people in need of urgent care, but can't afford it."

"It is very impressive. How much money do you have?"

"Enough, but this was built with donations from a lot of wealthy donors. I sold the idea of a completely private facility."

I was in awe. This place was impressive. We landed on the third floor. Tim had a welcoming committee at the door.

"Good morning, Tim, this must be Sam."

"Sam, this is Dr. Brady. Are the patients ready for us?"

"They are in the Sun room. I'll take you in and if you need anything, let me know."

The Sun room was large, open, and warm. Doug and Lori were sitting on couches facing the windows. There was a spectacular view of Mt. Rainier.

"Sam, its so nice to see you." Lori's smile was as wide as the room. Doug turned, but his face gave no comprehension.

"Lori, I'm glad that you're getting better. I would have been to see you sooner, but I had to wait until the mess was cleaned up."

"Doug, Sam came to see us."

"I wasn't sure that it was you. My memory is pretty bad. Between Pat hitting me on the head and the drugs she gave me, I'm a little foggy."

"That's one of the reasons that we came out today. Sam could you tell them what happened?"

I wasn't expecting to be the one to tell them the news, but they deserved to know what happened.

"Patricia attempted to kill me. She attacked me at Good Sam's. In the scuffle, she stabbed me and somehow fell on her knife. Unfortunately, she's dead. So, it is now safe for you two to go home."

"Really, we can go home. I've missed my son something fierce. Thank you, both."

"Now we've come to the second reason that we came. I want you both to know that your hospital bills are paid in full. We know that Doug will need a lot more therapy. The foundation that runs this clinic has decided to help with all of your bills and some living expenses for both of you."

"Wait, that's a lot to digest. This foundation is going to help us. They've paid our bills and after we go home help us some more."

"That's pretty much it. I know that this is a personal question, but are you and Doug going to stay together?"

"Yes, why?"

"Well, the foundation will need to know which house to update for Doug's needs. We'll get things started after you fill out these forms. Once things are started, Sam will be your contact with the foundation."

"Show me the papers. The sooner the better. I want to go home."

The papers were soon filled in. That's when Tim and I sat down to interview Lori, Doug sat in on the interview, but didn't add much to the process. We worked out a priority list of things that needed to be done. A decision was made to have them stay at her parents while the work was being completed. At the end of the day, it was decided to let them go home over the weekend. The work on the house would take at least two weeks. Tim approved the plans. I would check on them at least once a month, unless any problems arose.

On our drive back, Tim and I talked about my part in the work that the foundation would be doing. As we pulled into my driveway, Tim took a large file out. It was for me to look over. The file contained the terms of my employment. It seems that I now had a second job. The pay was very generous, hours were flexible, and I didn't have to quit my job. I was feeling invigorated. I hadn't noticed my shoulder since this morning.

When Jude got home, she asked how everything went.

"The day went well. The foundation is remodeling Lori's house to make it feasible to do Doug's therapy, plus add some more room. After paying the hospital bills, they'll receive a monthly allowance to live on. Tim has offered me a job as the foundation's representative in cases like this. I'll show you the job description and pay scale after dinner, plus I won't have to quit Good Sam's."

"How did you handle the long day?"

"I don't know what to say, but the shoulder hasn't bothered me all day. I don't know how long that will last."

"When do you plan to go back to work?

"If I feel okay, I might go in for a little bit tomorrow."

"Well, I guess that we'll play it by ear."

We had a very pleasant evening. Jude was impressed by the job. I was just happy to be sitting with my family.

I woke up with no discomfort in my shoulder. The sun was out beckoning me a return to normal. I decided to go in and see how I handled things. Knowing that they could and did handle the store when I'm gone, but I still needed to be there.

"Sam, let me know how you're doing. Try not to overdo it."

"I'll give it my best shot to not do anything stupid. I love you."

The Simone's went off to do whatever it is that we do. I was at work in a blur. The crew made a fuss over me as I came into the store. Linda gave me a tentative hug. I guess she was afraid of hurting me. We walked to my office.

"Sam, Tavin called. He wants you to call him. The number is on your desk."

"Thanks. Linda, I know it's only been a few days, but it feels good to be back."

"It feels good to have you back."

I sat down at my desk. A quick glance at my messages told me most could be dealt with later. Tavin's note was staring at me, so I gave him a call.

"Good morning, Tavin Long."

"Hey Tavin, Sam Simone returning your call."

"Great, I'm glad that you got back to me so soon. Is it possible to stop and see you this morning? I have something to go over with you."

"Sure, that would be fine. I'm at work. Come by anytime."

"I'll be there in fifteen minutes."

Right on the dot, Tavin knocked on my door.

"Come in. Have a seat. Would you like some coffee or pop?"

"A pop sounds good." I grabbed a cold soda out of my little cooler.

"What's up?"

"This has to do with the recent matter with The Good Samaritan national office. After their rogue employee's attack on you, plus the death of her supervisor and the assaults on Doug and Lori Smalls. They reached out to me to right the harm that you suffered at the hands of their employee."

"What are you telling me?"

"Sam as your lawyer, I negotiated a settlement on your behalf. The settlement covers your injuries and harm. If you except this settlement you agree not to sue them or hold them responsible. I have the terms of the settlement with me. We can look them over and you can make adjustments before we sign them."

I was dumbfounded.

"Let's take a look and see what they say."

We spent the next hour or so going over the documents. This was a serious amount of money. It would make a lot of my financial worries go away. My brain was on overdrive. When we had gone over the papers backwards and forwards, I looked at Tavin to ask a question.

"Let me ask you a couple of things. First, how much is your fee?"

"They are paying me fee. This all goes to you."

"Wow, now I want to set up money for Jude and the kids, for school and whatever. After paying my outstanding debts, I want the rest put into an account to be for our retirement."

"That is all doable. Once we sign the papers, I'll make the rest happen."

"Tavin, this is a dream come true. Thank you."

"Sam, you've given me so much. Cindy and I are getting married. You got me out of the clutches of Scooter's family. My life is finally going in the right direction, thanks to you."

www.ingramcontent.com/pod-product-compliance
Lightning Source LLC
Chambersburg PA
CBHW061516120726
48001CB00004B/1336